Praise for the 13 Reasons for Murder Series

"…hard to put down and am keen to read the next in the series."—Reader's Favorite 5-Star

"Full of sass, good friends, and a bit of blood, this novel was a joy to read."—Julie E.

"…suspenseful, addictive…hope there are more books with this character."—BookBub Review

"I look forward to…learning more about Britney."—Studiohnh.com Review

"…oddly addictive…cannot wait for the next book…"—Amazon.ca Review

"…flows at a quick pace and leaves you wanting more…"—Goodreads Review

"The plot is fresh and unique, a nice change to read something a little different…"—Reader's Favorite 4-Star

"…well written and kept me on the edge of my seat…"—Heather W.

13 Reasons for Murder: Politeness Kills

13 Reasons for Murder #1

Amanda Byrd

Blacksheep Press

Contents

About the
Author

Amanda Byrd is obsessed with fictional serial killers. From Patrick Bateman to Dr. Hannibal Lecter to Dexter Morgan and every butcher in between, Amanda loves figuring out what drives fiction's deadliest monsters. When she's not busy writing, Amanda can be found reading, playing video games, or watching shows and movies like Mindhunter, Hannibal, and Dexter. She lives in Florida with her bloodthirsty, flesh-eating cat . And her husband.

Follow Amanda online: www.amandabyrd.net
Sign up for the monthly email list and get a free story

Follow Amanda online:
Facebook: Author Amanda Byrd
Instagram: amanda_byrd_author
Goodreads: Amanda Byrd
Bookbub: Amanda Byrd

For Harvey, as always, for allowing—even pushing—me to
chase this crazy dream.

One

THE DAY WAS BREEZY but warm as I sat in my office, fielding phone calls from clients and emailing potential new hires for interviews. I was stuck at my desk, dumbfounded why when I could've been working at home on my patio, enjoying the weather, when the chimes of the door rang. I sighed and immediately realized why my assistant had taken the day off.

Standing from my chair, I straightened my skirt and checked myself out before walking out to greet the visitor. And I've got to say: I am hot. I stand five feet seven inches (without heels), with medium-length blonde hair and blue eyes so deep you'll lose yourself in them.

"H-hi," the twentysomething guy stuttered, sticking his hand out to shake.

I took his, smiled and shook firmly to his flimsy and clammy.

"I'm Alex—Alex Charles—and I was hoping you could help me." He rummaged through his messenger bag for a folder, took it out, and handed it to me.

I eyed him while he went through his bag, noting his ensemble from the bow tie down to the fun socks under his black dress pants to his freshly buffed black leather Oxfords to his short-sleeve button-down. He had black hair, blue eyes, and stood about six feet tall. I nodded as I accepted the résumé.

Alex fidgeted, shifting on his feet nervously as I read the paper over.

I looked up and smiled. "I can help you," I grinned. "Welcome to Passing Through Temp Agency, Alex. If you'll come to the cubicle over here," I walked toward the three cubicles on the opposite side of the door to my office and pulled out a chair for him. I motioned for him to sit, and he did, taking his bag off and setting it on the floor next to the chair.

"Here is where you fill out all your information. If you don't have your bank information, that's okay; we can put it in later. I'll need you to enter your résumé information, too"—I handed it back to him—"simply for matching purposes. Once you're finished, let me know, and we can continue getting you set up."

Alex nodded, handing the résumé back to me. "I have other copies if you need this one back."

That's bold of him, yet polite and thoughtful. I'm not sure, but I already get the feeling this kid is going to annoy the shit out of me just with how polite he is.

"That won't be necessary, but thank you. I'll take it back when you're done here."

I turned and walked—that strut I had—into my office.

Alex watched me—drooling, I was sure—as I went. I had that cheerleader walk, where my hips moved back and forth in seductive swing, and if my skirt had been a cheerleader skirt, it would've bounced like a tennis player getting ready to serve.

Alex wiped his mouth and tried to stop blushing the best he could and turned back to the computer to fill out all the forms required, watch an orientation video, and accept the terms of employment.

This was a temp agency, and he could possibly be without a job for weeks at a time, or at the end of an assignment, the client could choose to keep him on as their employee. It was a risk he was willing to take. He was desperate. He hadn't had a decent job in over a year. His state unemployment ended six months ago, and even then it barely paid the rent, and he was tired of asking his parents for money all the time. He wanted his independence back. Besides, he figured he was an exemplary employee, very valuable to the right company, and could easily be kept on by any of my clients. He'd done his homework and asked around to find out more about who my clients were—big-name doctors and lawyers were the majority of who came up, so Alex knew he'd be a perfect fit somewhere soon.

Forty minutes later, he was finished and stood, picking up his bag as he did, and turned to face my half-closed door. He rapped his knuckles lightly on the doorframe.

"Come in," came my muffled reply.

He pushed the door open, and I looked up at him. Not quite attractive but not ugly, he was an okay-looking guy.

I wondered if he had a girlfriend, maybe ever, given how polite and kind he came off. Women didn't really appreciate those things about men until it was too late.

"Please sit." I stood and motioned to the chair across the oak desk from me.

Alex did as he was asked, again setting his bag on the floor, then crossing his legs, setting clasped hands on his knee. He cleared his throat, appearing to want to speak, or maybe it was to break the uncomfortable silence.

I put my hand out for his résumé, which he handed me excitedly, and the sheet cut my finger.

"I'm so sorry, Ms. Cage! Ohmygod, I'm so, so sorry!" He furiously looked around for a tissue or paper towel as I pulled a drawer open and pulled out a box of tissues, setting them on the desk as I plucked one from the box for my cut.

I smiled. "It's okay. It's a simple paper cut."

Alex relaxed a little, though now he was more nervous than when he walked in.

"Would you like some water?"

He shook his head. "No, thank you."

"Okay, then. Let's get started so we can get you working ASAP."

Thirty minutes later, I had set a start date of next Monday for Alex to go work at one of the top surgeons' offices in the city. I may have been torturing the man with it being a plastic surgery facility, but his skills fit, and I wasn't about to pass up getting someone in there now. They wouldn't stop hounding me for a temp, yet they said they were "so busy we can barely answer the phones." My ass they were, but I'd get a full report from Alex at the end of the week.

We shook hands, and he left, sweating profusely through his excitement.

I guess he still felt really bad because he'd started sweating as soon as he saw the blood. I hoped he wasn't the blood-shy type. That wouldn't go over well in a surgeon's office, paper pusher or not.

He tried apologizing again on his way out, and I shooed him off. The phone started to ring just as the door chime sounded. I shook my head and let it go to voice mail. I was packing up and finishing the day from home.

Two

I KICKED MY SHOES off as soon as I got home after playing vehicular ping-pong in the afternoon Tampa traffic. I didn't live terribly far from the office, only a few miles, but a few miles turned into a half hour or more rather quickly and painfully.

I was lost in still-lingering traffic grievances and how much I wished the city and county could do more about them, when I heard a pitiful meow at my feet. I looked down to see my tiny girl, M—short for Minion of Darkness—looking quite perturbed. Apparently, one of my shoes had scared her from her perch in the window, and now it was Mommy's duty to pacify the princess. I petted her and sat down on the couch, taking my work laptop out as well as some folders, including Alex's.

"First, Mommy changes. Then, we go sit outside," I said to M and scratched her chin.

I went to my bedroom and threw on a pair of lounge shorts and a long-sleeve T-shirt. It may have been warm, but that breeze made me chilly. I'm an anomaly, what can I say?

I then opened all the windows to let some fresh air in. February is a fussy month here, and I was taking full advantage of it. M followed me around, yelling at me for Mommy time. She even jumped on top of my folders, scattering them everywhere. I simply shook my head. I'd have to rearrange them once I got outside.

I opened the sliding glass door to the screened-in patio and placed my work on the table, pulling up a chair, too. Sitting down, I sighed and giggled, beginning to sort through the mess M created. Employee files were no longer in order; I had to sort papers back into their homes in the correct folders before I could get back to my tedium of data entry. Normally, my assistant, Julie, did all this crap, but as I said, she had taken the day off. *Oh well, sometimes you have to do the things you hired others for when you're a small-business owner.*

I'd finally sorted everything when my cell phone rang. I didn't recognize the number—when did I ever, honestly—which meant it was probably one of my temps. I hit the green Answer button.

"Passing Through Temp Agency. Britney speaking. How can I help you?" I tried hard to sound like I wasn't annoyed and hoped it came through.

"Oh, uh, I'm glad I got you. I went back to the office, but the lights were out, and the door was locked. I had another question about starting on Monday. Oh by the way, this is Alex. Alex Charles? You just hired me maybe an hour ago?"

"Hi, Alex. What can I do for you?"

"Well, I was wondering…It's a surgeon's office…Do I need scrubs or…"

"Shit! Ahem, excuse that. I can't believe we didn't go over that. I'm very sorry, Alex. The doctor likes when you're professionally dressed the first day; then he'll tell you what color scrubs to get and where. He's got an account with one of the stores, and his people get discounts. It's very important when you go to the store you tell them you're temping for him. They have the colors he requires on file. The man's a little OCD and likes his people color-coded by job function."

Alex was silent on the other end, as those I sent to this particular surgeon usually were at this point in the conversation. Then he spoke up. "Okay. Professional. Does that mean suit and tie and jacket?"

"Yes," I replied, "a jacket is a must, or he'll freak out on you and call me pitching a bitch fit. I want a good report about you, Alex. I know you can do this. Oh, one last thing: Be assertive. Don't be afraid to speak up to coworkers, to me, or to the doctor. He's not as bad as he seems, just a little eccentric. Anything else?"

"No."

"Well, then let me get back to work, and I look forward to hearing from you next Friday. Remember, good reports, Alex. I picked you for this because I know you'll do well. Have a good rest of your day." I tried to smile through the phone.

"You, too, Ms. Cage. Thanks again."

He hung up, and I tossed my phone onto the table next to the laptop. I wanted to learn more about Alex, and that meant some social-media scouring before I started the data entry. I checked all the popular sites but couldn't find him anywhere.

Did he have friends? He mentioned his parents but not in a tone that would suggest they'd miss him if he went to the Dominican Republic and was kidnapped for an organ-harvesting operation. I almost felt bad for the guy, but maybe he liked it that way. So did I.

Pulling the stack of files closer, I opened the database to make sure all the information was up to date, like who was still available, on which assignments, emergency contact info, all the boring little tidbits that made up everyone's lives. *The devil is in the details,* I smirked.

Going through the files, I realized how many of my temps didn't really have anyone, not even an emergency contact in town. I wanted to feel bad, and I guess I did in some weird way, but I didn't let it bother me. They knew I was just a phone call away, but they also knew I wasn't their bestie.

The last folder was Alex's. I went through it slowly, reading everything printed out, taking it all in. His parents lived in Ocala, which was only a few hours' drive from Tampa, but he didn't have much else. A couple odd jobs between high school and graduating college, then onto work in one of the local hospitals as a nurse.

I was puzzled. Why would a nurse want to become a paper pusher? What had he seen that messed him up so badly? Maybe one day I'd ask him, but today wasn't it. As I finished entering his personal information, I giggled, a wry grin on my face. I entered his assignment, Dr. Osten, and saved the data.

As I closed my laptop, I grinned again. "Oh, Alex Charles, what have you gotten yourself into?"

Three

As a single woman, I didn'tcook much, but when I do, it's usually a whole big to-do for friends. Tonight, however, I wanted pasta in a creamy garlic sauce, and I wanted to eat it on my patio with a glass of red wine, watching the sun set. I was wearing comfy clothes, and considering I'm a bit of a messy cook, I knew I needed to do something about it. I also wanted to keep what I had on relatively clean. The combination of pasta sauce and me wasn't that. Pushing my chair back, I stood and picked up my pile of work and put it back in my bag in the living room, then trotted off to find a longer T-shirt that I didn't mind getting gross. It was hot, but I was always most comfortable in sweats.

By the time M stopped her sunbathing and realized I was gone, she panicked, running into the house screaming for me. She found me as I was mid-leg-into-pant-leg and almost knocked me out of my precarious position. Luckily, she'd run past me and circled me a few times, allowing me to fully put my pants on. M pounced onto the bed and head-butted my thigh until I stopped to pet her.

"You're lucky you're so cute." I scratched her chin and ran my hand down her soft back.

She purred her acknowledgment, scowling as I walked away to change my shirt. She sat on the bed, statuesque, her eyes saying, "Bow to me, human." But as spoiled as I'd made her, I wasn't about to let her run my life.

In the kitchen, I shook her food container, and as usual, she came running. I'd already started the water to boil for the pasta, which it did, as I poured M's food. I caught it just before it boiled over onto my spotless ceramic cooktop—I'm superb at multitasking. I turned the heat down and poured the pasta in, letting it simmer before turning it off and letting the residual heat cook it. The sauce heated up quickly, like soup, so I simmered it before it bubbled too much and burned. I'm pretty particular about my pasta, when I do cook it, so I take the time and care I should.

I take the time and care necessary with a lot of things—my business, Julie when I trained her, nurturing business relationships, Minion…I don't really have plans or feelings beyond expanding my business to the point I won't have to be in the office every day. Since growing up, I'd never wanted children. I'd considered maybe eventually getting married, but my career meant too much to me to bother with all the courting. Besides, I don't have the patience or tolerance for that mess. All of my girlfriends have had their hearts broken this year, and I'm over here comforting them but not giving a shit that I just have a long-distance friend with benefits.

I pulled the lid off the pot of pasta to check the tenderness. Not too hard but not too soft—just the way I liked it. I drained it and poured it onto a plate, followed by the sauce. Then I poured a glass of red and set it on the table. Okay, so it wasn't exactly a red; it was red Moscato, but whatever. I liked it, and it seemed to go with everything, and it was great for parties.

That reminded me: I was overdue to throw one. I'd have to get Julie on the planning.

Julie, by the way, was my star. Not only was she my assistant at Passing Through, but she often asked for more responsibility. So, I gave her some other things to handle, like part of my social calendar to include business functions. She seemed to enjoy it, and ·she was pretty good at it, so I gave her a raise. She juggled the two so well, I was plotting to steal her from the office and ask her to be my personal assistant once I got busier, which I could see happening in the near future.

Julie had once told me that she grew up hearing things like she wasn't good enough, and that she'd never be worthy of anyone's respect, which explained why she'd been so mousy around me. What she didn't know was that I'd grown up the same, but I'd chosen a different way to handle the trauma. My heart truly went out to her; Julie was my trauma sister. I'd do whatever I could to show her that she was never that meek little girl.

I enjoyed my pasta and Moscato while M sat at my feet mewing as though asking for some, her pupils huge like the cartoon cats who intentionally looked sad when they wanted to guilt trip you.

Like any feline, Minion was razor sharp, and manipulative. She knew just what to do to make me stop working and spend the day cuddling with her—still another reason I didn't need a child or significant other.

I laughed. *Manipulated by an animal.* Man, was I a sucker. But only for M.

Sometimes, I fell for the manipulation from my friends, but they always did it in good fun or to try to surprise me. Which reminds me: I hate surprises. The first time they tried to surprise me, someone got a black eye. If you're asking if I felt bad about punching the male stripper who showed up at my door on my twenty-fifth birthday, the answer is no. I still don't feel bad. I know the guy was only doing his job, but well, he rang the wrong doorbell that night.

To say I lack empathy was inaccurate. I do feel things for others, though only for those I'm close to: my girlfriends, my father, Minion, and maybe my long-distance friend with benefits. I've been told I should go to therapy or a psychiatrist, but I disagree. I see nothing wrong with caring about only those in my immediate circle. If that made me a narcissist—check the definition; it didn't—then so be it. Simply put, it made me more of an asshole than anything else, I supposed. It's not that I chose not to care about the whole world; it's that I chose and valued my sanity over the stress caring about every little thing would cause.

I've been there, and it was awful. Gratefully, I pulled myself out of that emotional cesspool and traded it for the cool, calm, and collected "heartless" person everyone sees. Some people even liked that about me; others were jealous.

I savored the last forkful of my dinner and swished the remaining wine in the glass, lost in thought. Did I have any more work that needed to be done, or could I relax outside and read a book, purring cat on my lap? Finishing the wine, I washed everything I'd used to make dinner and put it in the dish rack to dry. I took a glass from the cabinet and poured some water from the filter pitcher, grabbed a book, and went to lie in the hammock I had in the corner of my screened-in patio. It was one of those you could get online with the metal stand so you didn't need trees to tie it to. It was the best I could do in my townhouse, and I was more than okay with that. Minion jumped up on my stomach as I opened the book, something about monsters and the people who hunt them. It had taught me a lot about guns in a fun way—much more fun than going to the range and asking one of the men (there were no women on the sales floor) who always were kind—though some looked at me as though I was just a dumb blonde—to teach me about this gun or that.

I did have friends who were knowledgeable about all sorts of weapons, but I preferred reading and solitude. I did have one girlfriend I went to the range with, and she was always honest with me about "if I'm going to buy one, I need to practice with it first," and I appreciate that. She was the only friend who didn't freak out I mentioned I have a few guns in the house. She agreed that I needed self-protection. That was the point in time I stopped telling the girls about my interest in weapons.

Hours went by, and I closed the book, finished and sat sfied. I woke Minion up, making her glare at me, and went to put the book on its shelf with the rest of the series, plucking another from my to-read pile and setting the bookmark just inside the cover. Glancing at the clock on the wall, I saw it was midnight, my favorite time of day. Some people were out and about, but not many, and it was cool enough to get a good jog in along Bayshore Avenue, one of the main drags here in town. I changed into dark gray running gear and locked up the house. Tonight, though, I wasn't planning to jog Bayshore.

Four

I JOGGED LIGHTLY, SLOWLY building sweat as it was a bit on the chilly side. I may have lived in Central Florida, but anything below eighty, and I was cold. Yet I slept with the thermostat at sixty-five. It was weird, I know. Somehow, I made it the five or so miles in about fifteen minutes. *Damn, I should slow down. And damn, he lives close.* I turned onto South Lorenzo and started walking, music down low enough to hear if anyone came up behind me, watching the apartments from the other side of the street, looking for which one was Alex's. I'd forgotten to look at his file before I left, but I found him rather easily, mope-walking down his side of the street. I ducked behind a large palm tree.

Alex walked up to a gorgeous, Spanish-inspired building that looked like something from a movie. I'd decided to research the building later. Not because I was interested, which I was, but because I needed the layout. That would also require a trip to the city offices downtown. No worries, I had contacts there from sending them temps.

He used a key to open the front door, and it closed behind him. I sat there watching, hoping his apartment wasn't on the back side of the building, when a light came on in a window on the second floor. Alex walked to that window and closed the shades.

Who leaves their shades open?

His shadow lingered. Maybe he felt he was being watched, or maybe he'd turned his back. I didn't know, and I didn't care. If he knew he was being watched, waiting a few more minutes was taking a big chance because the cops would come rolling up if Alex called them. But no, no cops. No cars at all, in fact. I waited until he turned the light out before I jogged back home.

Minion was on the stairs inside the door, not surprisingly glaring at me as she yawned. Then she yelled at me. I usually jogged in the morning, which she was used to, though she didn't like it any better than now. She hated when I left the house or even the room she was in. Like a human child, I supposed.

"Oh, hush," I said, bending slightly to scratch her chin and pet her. "Come on, let's get you some treats. Then I'm showering and going to bed."

M happily followed, scarfing down the three treats I gave her. I took my sneakers off and put them on the rack by the front door, double-checked to make sure I locked it, and turned out the lights downstairs as I headed up. The water always took a minute or two to heat up, so I'd started it before laying out my pajamas and clothes for the office tomorrow, then undressed and threw my towels over the glass wall.

Afterward, I hit Play on a movie and fell asleep, Minion in my hair, cuddling me.

The alarm went off all too early. It was my own fault for staying out so late, but I'd be fine. Coffee would be my savior today, and if it wasn't, there were always energy drinks. I didn't care to know what they did to the inside of my body, though I did know the carbonation helped to clean things, and people blew how bad they were for you severely out of proportion. Whatever. I had a workday to get through, and nothing was going to hinder my getting out on time. Dinner with the girls at the British pub was tonight's plans, and there was nothing and no one to stop me.

The phones rang off the hook today, and Julie was on top of it like cat fur on black clothes. I truly was grateful for her abilities. By lunch, she'd answered all the morning calls, sorted the incoming mail, and responded to every email that went to her.

After a hellish morning, she popped her head into my office to ask if I wanted her to grab me anything for lunch. I handed her a fifty and told her that her lunch was on me. She stopped saying no a while ago, so she nodded and smiled. I just want-ed a chicken Caesar salad, my go-to most days, whether Julie went out for it or I had lunch delivered. Julie even locked the door and set the phones to voice mail when she left. *Yeah, I definitely need her as a personal assistant when I move out of here and have someone take over. Unless she wants to take over…*

I unconsciously tapped my pen against my pursed lips. I only stopped when I noticed red on the top. Julie would be a good fit for my position. I'd noted to talk to her about it, without a date or time. The truth was I didn't know when I planned to leave and let someone else run the place for me. I'd have to think about that.

The door chime rang, signaling Julie was back.

"I'm back and headed to the kitchen. Meet you there!" she cheerfully called.

I smiled and looked at the mountain of paperwork I still had to finish before day's end. Sighing, I stood, straightened my skirt, and went to have lunch with Julie. Maybe I'd ask her what her life plans were beyond working for me; did she want more of a career or was she happy where she was?

By the time I got to the kitchen, Julie had silverware, napkins, and drinks all set out for us. I loved this girl so much.

"You kicked ass this morning," I said as I pulled out my chair and sat down.

She blushed. "Thanks." Julie didn't take compliments very well, and neither did I. I'd have to work on that with her.

"You remind me a lot of me. I still have a hard time taking compliments." I dug my fork into my salad.

"Really? You make it look so easy, so effortless." She bit into her burger.

"Precisely." I winked. "I make it *look* easy. I'll teach you if you want."

" Could you please?" She blushed a little at asking for help. Also a lot like me.

"I'm not CPR certified anymore, so please do us both a favor and don't choke on your burger," I poked at her.

We both laughed. Our conversation led to what our plans for the night were and if we really wanted to attend our set gatherings.

I did; hell yeah. I hadn't seen the girls in almost a month from being bogged down by professional events and other "hobbies." No one knew about those though. Hell, I'd just figured out I had a new fun-time activity. This was going to take away from my weekend trips to my benefits, but I could live with it provided no one suspected anything and my benefit buddy was cool with it. He was usually cool with anything, but I didn't exactly want to give him the impression I was dating. I shuddered at the thought.

Julie and I finished our lunches, cleaned up, and were back at our desks by one o'clock on the dot. Damn, we made a great team. Maybe I would talk to Julie sooner than later about her career path. She already knew most of the clients from tagging along as my plus-one to events.

As she left for the day, I teased her one last time. "Don't party too hard," I giggled.

"Oh yes. A bottle of wine and Netflix with my cat," she laughed and waved on her way out.

I pressed the power button on my monitor as I stood, gathering my things to go home, change, and meet the girls, when my cell phone rang.

"Hello?"

"Ms. Cage? It's Alex."

Five

I DROVE HOME A little on the angry side. How had he gotten my cell number, anyway? *Oh right, dumbass. It's on your business card.* He said he called because he wanted to double-check his assignment, but I was pretty sure that was a lie. It felt more like he wasn't sure how to flirt, which would've been wrong anyway. I was his employer, for fuck's sake. He was probably feeling me out to see if I was that kind of woman. *What a ballsy little prick he is!* Multitudes of names ran through my head, but I still couldn't get over the gall this kid had to even think of flirting with me. I was sure he'd had at least one girlfriend in his life. He was smart, responsible, not my kind of cute, but someone's. And, to top it off, if he could be any more polite and sweet, I was positive he'd give me a cavity. I think that's what drove me so crazy and led me to planning to kill him.

When I got home, I tore up the stairs, changed into a nice pair of pants and a shirt, and kept on the heels I'd been wearing all day. After feeding Minion—who, as usual, was judging me for leaving her—I went right back out the door and locked it. I slowed to a more normal walk to my SUV, to avoid questions later from the nosy old bitch across the street, and got in.

I loved this car almost as much as I loved Minion. A 2019 Jeep Wrangler Unlimited, black on black, lifted three inches. I'd intended to have more work done to it so I could rock crawl with it, but I needed to learn how to navigate the terrain first. Good thing I had an old friend who Jeep-crawled often and offered to teach me. I'd have to go north for it, but it was so worth it. Bucket list item to be checked off soon.

There was little traffic headed north to meet the girls, which was strange. Five o'clock meant rush hour, especially headed north, as most people worked in St. Pete or downtown. I took it for what it was, a chance to make great time to the restaurant.

I valeted my Jeep and put my name on the wait list—there were seven of us, so we'd have a table upstairs. One by one, the girls arrived, and by the time there were five of us, we were given the okay to go up to our table. Sarah, Danielle, Kristen, and Heather were chatting away as I ordered two bottles of merlot and a cheese sampler to start us off. As our server, Rachel, walked away, Kate and Colleen reached the top of the stairs breathlessly. I stood, greeting each of them with a kiss on the cheek.

"Why are you two so out of breath?"

They looked at each other and laughed. "We decided to race from the valet to here. Risking broken or twisted ankles in heels," Kate huffed.

I laughed, and the girls all stood up for greetings and cheek kisses. By the time Rachel brought out all seven glasses, both bottles, and the cheese sampler, we'd all finally taken our seats. No one bothered to look at the menu while Rachel was gone, so we asked her for a few more minutes and another bottle of merlot. Three would be good for seven of us, right?

We toasted to it being the first night in a while we were able to get together, all of us having busy professional lives, half of us parents, too. I loved spending time with my nieces and nephews, but I also very much enjoyed giving them back. Kids just weren't for me, and my friends respected that. But enough about me.

I suggested we all decide what we were eating before Rachel came back. That girl was always so good to us, and we were good to her. So much so that we'd even invited her out with us on more than one occasion; however, even though she planned to join us, she inevitably got called into work. And since her apartment was on the pricey side, like every other decent rental in Tampa, she took the shift.

Rachel came back a minute or two later, making her way around the table, taking our orders. A creature of habit, I ordered the fish and chips. They were the closest I'd ever had to the real thing. Ever since my trip to Britain, I compared *everything* the Americans made to the real food. Some of it was horrific, some tolerable, most nowhere close. But then there were the rare times when it was spot on, and here, this pub was spot on. Colleen pulled me from my thoughts, asking me what I'd been up to lately. *Oh, nothing. Just stalking a new hire.* I sipped my wine and shook my head.

"Not much," I said, setting the glass down, "just working like a dog to make the dream a reality."

Everyone laughed. They rarely admitted it, but every last woman at that table was jealous of me. I'd succeeded—finally—at starting my own company, I had a receptionist, I was never stuck in a tight spot between kids and spouses because I had neither. I was what they all wanted to be and couldn't.

I was never cocky about it, though. I always remembered where I came from and who had helped me along the way. And I always helped them back, as well as helping other newbies as much as I could before I'd have to join a mentoring program or something. A few of the girls had brought me their interns with the most promise, and I had groomed them the same way I wanted to groom Julie, who didn't need much more help other than learning to accept compliments.

Our food arrived, and we toasted again, digging in as if none of us had eaten anything all day. In truth, we all probably had salads for lunch because we knew we'd be fed well at dinner.

My fish and chips were delicious, like always. The kitchen would always send a few extra fish out for me, too, which was sweet. I think I'd go so far as to say that we were friends with everyone there, including the owner. He'd hit on me once or twice before, and I shut him down every time. I don't do married men. Okay, not this close to home.

He and his family lived not far from me in south Tampa, and I really didn't see the reason in destroying a perfectly good professional relationship. His wife, Nancy, was a client of mine. She was a pediatrician who always accepted those fresh out of college looking to gain their first couple years of experience and move on to their own practices. While her own practice benefitted from continual infusions of fresh talent trained on the latest techniques, Nancy saw her mentoring as a public service, churning out gifted doctors in a state that was desperate for them.

On a personal level, Nancy and I got along well, though she preferred talking to Julie rather than me. I suspected she either knew of her husband's flirtation, or she felt threatened by me. I was ten years her junior, and I still had the body of an eighteen-year-old I try not to downplay my looks, but I'm not cocky, either. I'm pretty, sure, and there are much prettier and classier women out there. I don't understand why men always think I'm the one who wants to be charmed or something. Most of them are full of shit, anyway.

Rachel came back around as we finished our meals, bringing three more bottles of merlot and pulling out her writing pad, asking if we wanted dessert. I sure did, and nothing would hit the spot quite like a nice fat slice of cheesecake. The others agreed, so we ordered a whole cheesecake with raspberry sauce on the side. It arrived precut, and Rachel handed us all dessert plates and forks. She even gave us individual ramekins with raspberry sauce. We needed nothing else and passed the plates around for our slices. I was the designated person to dole them out, having been the one to organize the gathering in the first place, which also allowed me to save the best piece for last, for me. We enjoyed the cheesecake and finished the wine.

Rachel knew us well enough to split the checks as evenly as possible. We paid, took care of her, and said our "see you soons"—we didn't say goodbye because it wasn't forever, maybe a few months, but not forever.

Six

I BACKED INTO MY driveway around ten-ish. I was exhausted, mentally and physically. I hoped I wasn't coming down with something. Maybe it was just today and all that sitting I'd done. I rarely sat down for more than an hour at a time. I couldn't; I'm fidgety and prefer to stand or pace. I got to thinking about Alex again and how he'd called under the pretense of "double-checking for Monday." That really irritated me. It wasn't an emergency, yet he'd chosen to call after hours, even being so polite about it and apologizing profusely. I saw right through that act, and as much as I wanted to text him, I shut my truck off, got out, locked and armed it, and unlocked my front door. I froze at what I saw at my feet.

Flowers and a card. What the fuck was going on here? I squatted down to pick them up and pulled the card. On the front was a teddy bear holding a heart that had the words *I'm Sorry* on it. I opened it, skimmed past the lame two-line sentiment to the handwritten part, and read:

Dear Ms. Cage,

Please forgive my calling after hours and not having an emergency reason to do so. I deeply regret any anger, annoyance, or inconvenience I may have caused you.

Sincerely,

Alex Charles

This was getting out of hand. Now he knew where I lived? I'd have to call the phone company tomorrow and have my landline and address unlisted.

I opened the door, dropped my purse on the couch, and threw the flowers in the trash. I didn't want to call the cops. I didn't want anyone else involved. Period. I'd already made plans for Alex that he wasn't aware of and wouldn't be until they happened.

I flashed a wicked smile to myself there in the dark, fond of my hobby. Sure, it was messy, but so was anything worthwhile in life. Family, relationships, school; it was all messy in one way or another. Hell, my company got messy from time to time I fucking *hated* when my company gets messy and will do *anything* to fix it. I'm not above blackmail and threats, and my clients know this. Only a few of them have experienced it, and I didn't feel bad—they're not going to talk shit about me and trash my honest reputation because we had a spat over cost, hell no. So, the way I see it, they got what they deserved, and I got my public apology.

As for Alex, like I said, I had plans for him, and his dropping flowers by my house as an apology wasn't in those plans. It was now time to revise and definitely not a problem. I jogged every day, sometimes twice when I was angry. I was angry thinking about his stupid flowers, so I went upstairs to change and jog by Alex's place.

Once I got there, I was surprised by the lack of security. There weren't any cameras, and only the main door locked. I slipped an envelope with his name on it between the door and the frame, sure someone would notice it once they opened the door and left. I'd also had my face covered in a ski mask in the case of cameras I'd missed or nosy neighbors.

I turned and jogged the opposite way I came from, again, in case of nosy neighbors.

I undressed and showered when I got home and crawled into bed with Minion. I lay there, blankly watching the news in a vain effort to prepare for tomorrow's weather. It would change; it was the time of year most states called winter. We called it "maybe spring" because the weather got really temperamental with deciding if it wanted to be hot or cold. Regardless, I knew one thing about February in Florida: I would always need long sleeves or a jacket. I'm *that* person. I transplanted from the northern states a few years ago, but anything under eighty and I was cold.

But I also needed cold to sleep. Outside was a perfect fifty degrees, so I had the ceiling fan on and windows open. Minion was not happy with her tiny, cold paws. The weather called for more of the same the rest of the week. It wasn't entirely unusual, but I'd take it because soon we'd all be bitching about how miserable and gross the heat and humidity and rain were.

I rolled over to cuddle Minion and help keep her warm. The red light of the alarm clock said one o'clock in the morning. I really had to stop this, or I was actually going to start needing some kind of eye cream at night to get rid of the bags that were starting to form under my eyes.

Wednesday, six a.m., and that obnoxious beeping sound. I slammed the Off button and begrudgingly got out of bed. It was evident I'd gotten up on the wrong side of it. I was immediately drenched in thoughts of Alex and how surprisingly angry I was that he'd crossed not one but two lines in the same day. I planned to set aside time to call him into the office and explain that it was inappropriate.

Then I smirked, remembering the cheesy note I'd left made from letters cut out of a magazine. "Leave Britney alone, or

I'll come for you" was all it read. Let the kid think I have a crazy boyfriend. I cackled and got ready for my day.

I called Alex as soon as I got comfortable at my desk. He answered on the second ring, sounding groggy.

"Alex, it's Ms. Cage. I'm sorry if I woke you, but I need you to come into the office. I lost your direct deposit paperwork. I think I accidentally shredded it. Can you be here at 1:15?"

I heard shuffling on the other end of the line before he answered.

"Yeah. I mean yes, I can be there at 1:15."

"Great. I'll double check the shredder, too, just to make sure it didn't get thrown away in the regular trash. Can't be too safe these days. See you soon." I hung up.

Julie slid her chair over to my open door. "Who did you just lie to and why?"

I launched into Alex being creepy, and she agreed the lie was necessary to get him in front of me for a conversation and not under the pretense of him thinking he was already in trouble. He was; I simply didn't want him to know until he'd shown up. There's no sense in making someone worry and causing unnecessary anxiety and panic over something that can be handled with a white lie. Now I actually had to shred his direct deposit information, so I did and went about the rest of the morning.

By the time Alex showed up, I'd shredded his information and pulled it back out as proof. Maybe I was being overly cautious, but with this guy now knowing where I lived, this couldn't be anything other than me plainly drawing a line and marking boundaries. Chimes ringing, he came in the door, and Julie greeted him. She checked with me if she could send him in.

I nodded.

As he crossed through the doorway, I asked him to close the door. He started visibly shaking. Only he knew why because I sure didn't care. I would be nice yet firm, caring but aloof. No sending mixed signals but drawing very permanent boundaries.

He sat down, handing me the voided check, and I handed him the paper to fill out. The process took less than three minutes. He handed me the form back.

"Is that all?"

"Actually, no, it's not," I said, crossing my ankles under the desk, hands in my lap.

Alex uncrossed his legs and, knees together, began to nervously bounce his right leg. "Am I in trouble?"

"I wouldn't say trouble, but you did cross a few boundaries last night, and we need to clear that up. Now. I honestly almost called the cops last night I was so frightened by what you did."

He started to protest, and I held a hand up.

"Now, I know you did it for good reasons, and I accept your apology. However, you need to understand, and respect, that my cell phone number is only to be used in emergency situations, true emergencies, like you're in the hospital or something along those lines. My house is 100 percent *off limits*."

Alex mumbled his apology and promised never to do it again and that he didn't want a police record.

I stood and extended a hand.

Alex stood, and his shaking grew worse.

"Again, I'm *really* sorry," he squeaked.

"Let's just call this a misunderstanding. Know if anything like it happens again, I will press charges."

Alex turned and walked out, opening the door with his head hung in embarrassment. He said bye to Julie, and the chimes told me he was gone.

Julie came into my office and sat on the chair Alex had just vacated.

"Well?"

"I put the fear of a police record for stalking and trespassing in him." My grin belying what would positively happen, regardless of boundaries.

Seven

THE DAY ENDED WITH no further drama. I invited Julie over for dinner seeing as how neither of us had plans and there was a show we talked about watching together. She agreed but wanted to run home first to feed her cat and change. We had parted for what would be an hour when she rang my doorbell. I opened the door wearing sweatpants, a long-sleeve T-shirt, and fuzzy slippers. Julie laughed as I let her in. She took her sweater off revealing she was wearing the same, only with leggings instead of sweats. We laughed, and I offered her a drink.

"I've got red Moscato, merlot, or I can make us dirty martinis," I said.

"I haven't had a good martini in a while," she responded.

I went to work adding ice to the shaker, then vodka, and finally, olive juice. Before shaking, I skewered two olives on those little plastic swords and placed them in each glass. Then I shook and poured. I brought the drinks out and set them on coasters on the glass coffee table.

Julie was the only employee of mine I'd allowed myself to cross boundaries with. She reminded me a lot of myself, and we had become fast friends. We even cat-sitted for each other. We got to talking about the show we were about to start watching. It turned out she'd read the book, and I had yet to. We also got to talking about what to order for dinner. Cheeseburgers came out of both of our mouths at the same time.

"Jinx! You owe me a Coke," Julie laughed.

"More like I owe you a promotion or raise," I said.

"One day," she said, "but not right now. That Alex kid…"

"Don't worry about him. He's on my leash now and won't be getting off anytime soon. And I'm not planning to leave the office anytime soon, so you have time to decide if taking my position is what you really want."

Julie blushed and thanked me, raising her glass in a toast.

"To friendship and the best boss a girl could ever hope for."

I pulled the menus of three different burger joints, and Julie chose which one. We decided our order and I called to place it. Hanging up the phone, I looked at Julie. "Forty-five minutes." She nodded her acceptance.

Julie turned the TV on as I took our glasses into the kitchen and made more. She had the show ready to go by the time I came back and sat down. We clinked glasses, sipped, and Julie pressed Play.

Dinner arrived just before the episode ended. It really was perfect timing. We could continue to watch the series and eat at the same time. I grabbed some place mats, plates, silverware, and napkins, and we enjoyed our dinner while yelling at the characters on the screen. Between episodes, we talked about how much we liked the casting and how great the story was.

We'd gotten through three episodes before nine when Julie decided she had to leave. I walked her to the door, thanked her for coming, and hugged her.

"Text me when you're home."

"Yes, Mom," Julie joked.

She got in her Toyota sedan and backed out of the drive-way, waving as she pulled away. I closed the door and made sure everything was cleaned up before I went upstairs to change for my jog.

Maybe jogging at night was better; however, I preferred the bustle of Bayshore in the early morning hours before work. But I couldn't properly stalk—or research, or as I preferred to call it—in the mornings. Too much light, too many people, more cops on the road. Nighttime was the best, and I'd have to adjust for my hobby.

I took my jog and watched again until he turned his lights out. I was careful not to be caught each time, but something in the back of my brain gnawed away at me, telling me I needed to stop watching every night because I *would* get caught if I didn't slow down. I didn't want to slow down, but what more could I learn from watching every single night? The guy had no life! Maybe he had a pet frog or a serious porn addiction that kept him indoors or something, but he had no social life, no family here…nothing.

I jogged home, showered, and went to sleep.

Thursday, the week was almost over, but that damned beep-ing from my alarm clock made me pissy. *I should probably either start using my phone or use the radio part, but I really don't do FM radio.* All I could figure was that it was either that noise causing my horrible wake-up mood or my late-night jogs. Good thing those were about to stop for a while and my research could take on other forms. I grinned, petted Minion, and walked a little lighter to the bathroom. Minion followed me in and batted at me through the shower curtain. Either

she was mad I hadn't fed her yet, or she was feeling playful. Half the time I couldn't tell. She had resting bitch face like most cats do, just like her human mommy.

I turned the showed off and was in the middle of drying myself off when Minion connected with bare leg. It hurt almost as bad as cutting myself shaving. I got out, cleaned it with witch hazel, and covered it.

Looking down at Minion, I giggled. I couldn't be mad; she was playing. Now, if she'd tried to play with my eyelid, I would have been mad and really would have had to be concerned about cat-scratch fever and go to the ER, and I *hated* the ER. The bandage would hold for at least half the day, and there were more in the office since federal laws required me to have a first aid kit. No white pants, I told myself and laughed. I owned exactly one pair of white pants, and they were skinny jeans, which I wouldn't be caught dead in at the office during working hours. A casual business dinner? Sure, with heels and a nice top. I worked hard to get where I'm at, and I'm not going to be sloppy and ruin my stellar reputation over that.

I finished getting ready for the day and fed Minion before I left. Traffic was back to normal—it sucked, but at least I was able to listen to a lot of good tunes before parking at the office. I got out of my Jeep, singing and skipping in the door.

Julie looked panicked. She'd never seen me so loose in a professional environment, only when it was just us or when we were out with the girls. I kept singing my way into my office and hung my jacket on the hanger on the back of the door. Setting my bag down on its table, I sat in my chair and turned my monitor on—and screamed.

Julie came running in. "Ohmygod, are you okay?"

My jaw hung open, and I pointed. I couldn't make a sound.

Eight

THERE ON THE SCREEN was a huge spider. It was an image, but regardless, it scared the shit out of me. I also hated spiders and snakes, on top of hating the ER. I tried to figure out who had access to my computer when the office was closed, and the only people who came to mind were the cleaners and Julie. The cleaners knew better than to do something like this, and Julie did text me when she got home last night. But she *was* here before me today. Before I could say anything or begin questioning her, Julie burst into hysterical laughter.

"Don't cry now; you might ruin your makeup," I venomously commented.

Julie was laughing so hard she couldn't speak. She clutched her sides and stomach with her arms making what looked like an X. =I shooed her out with my hand, and she stumbled a bit, making me giggle. I'd get over this trick, but I'd need at least an hour.

I changed my desktop back to an image of abstract art and carried on with my day. The day was starting at a snail's pace and didn't pick up by lunch. I'd thought about going home and maybe taking a nap or doing more research, but I couldn't think of much more to do during the daylight.

I still didn't know if Alex drove or took the bus and felt the hot flash of anger at not asking. Dr. Osten validated for his regular employees but not for temps, which I didn't find fair, but I understood it. He paid them well enough to compensate for the ten-dollar-fee for the whole day. I didn't necessarily feel bad for Alex, but I did want to let him know, so I searched the database for his number and called him.

"Hello?"

"Hi, Alex, Britney Cage. I couldn't remember if we'd talked about how you get around, if you drive or take the bus, and I wanted to call you before you start with Dr. Osten."

"Oh, I take the bus for now. My car's in the shop, and I won't have it back for another week or so."

"Okay, well, the garage near Osten's office is ten dollars daily, and he doesn't validate except for his employees, and I wanted you to know."

"Thanks, Ms. Cage, but I think I'll be taking the bus. It's cheaper. I'll only drive if I have to."

"Then it's settled. Make us look good, Alex, and I'll talk to you next week."

I didn't give him a chance to say anything else before hanging up. It was lunch time, and I found myself not very hungry. So, for an hour, I watched Netflix. *That* was my research for the day. There were so many things to choose between there and Prime, I'd made handwritten lists of what else to watch at home. Julie called my extension when she got back from lunch, hearing a man's voice and not wanting to interrupt. I turned it off, noting what time on the counter I'd left off.

"Do I hear a man in there with you?"

"You did, but it was just a movie."

Julie sounded deflated. "Oh, I was hoping it was someone secret who you might—"

I hung up.

Julie rolled her chair over to the open door. "What," she laughed, "I just want to see you happy."

"Okay, crazy cat lady, I'll make you a deal. When you start dating, so will I." I didn't mean a word I said, even had my fingers crossed under the desk.

Julie thought about it for a minute. "You're on! I've been talking to this guy on MatchMe, and we were thinking to meet up this weekend."

I scowled. "I lied. I had my fingers crossed. You go on your date. I'm fine, really. I'm happy with not having to take care of anyone else aside from me and Minion."

"Fine," Julie huffed, "have it your way then."

I laughed and looked around my desk for something, any-thing, work-related to do, but couldn't find anything. This was the problem when you were too efficient.

Screw this, I was going shopping. I turned my computer off, grabbed my bag, and told Julie I was leaving for the day. She didn't ask why, and I loved that about her. She never asked unless I looked like death had touched me. In my Jeep, I found my favorite party song channel and blared it, dancing as I drove.

I parked outside Macy's, like always, and marched to the beat in my head. My credit card companies would love me today.

I backed into my driveway around nine-thirty. My Jeep is a four door, which was a good thing because I spent a lot of money. I managed to take all the bags out at the same time without falling over or ripping any. Getting the front door open was another story and a bit of a disaster. I ripped three bags—nothing of super significant importance inside—and nothing was damaged. Leaving my heels at the front door, I took all the bags upstairs and came back down to lock up and feed Minion. My poor baby girl was feeling rather neglected, and she told me by yelling at me. I gave her extra treats and promised to be home with her all night tomorrow night and all weekend.

I turned the lights out as I went back up, sorting things to be dry cleaned or washed and others for my hobby. Inside my closet was a small door hidden behind my clothes. I'd turned it into a safe once I'd gotten my second pistol, a Gen 4 Glock 23 .40-caliber. It was my favorite. My Shield EZ .380 was by my bedside and was my carry weapon of choice. I had knives hidden in the Jeep and one in my purse, too. A lady couldn't be too well protected.

The safe was large enough to hold my hobby supplies also. I was an organizational nut, not that you could tell by looking at the disaster my bedroom was, but that was beside the point. I placed the supplies in their respective homes and closed the safe. It beeped, telling me it locked.

I changed and turned toward the bed to see Minion staring at me plaintively. I petted her, immediately soothing her, and we went to sleep, she in my hair, my arms around her like she was a stuffed animal. After all, she was like one when we slept, though I had no plans to kill her. I loved her too much for that.

Nine

FRIDAY AND THE REST of the weekend came and went. I didn't do much aside from cleaning, laundry, binge watching shows, and imagining. I imagined so much, so many things. I tried to imagine life with a boyfriend or husband, and that ended messier than my hobby usually did. Then I tried to imaging life with a husband and a kid. That would put me in an even bigger mess. Finally, I just imagined Alex Charles in a white room. I let my mind take over, and the room changed colors from white to blue to black, yellow, green, orange, and finally red. I smiled and opened my eyes, deciding to catch up on the reading I'd put aside for so long. I read for a few hours until I'd finished one of the five I'd started and decided to pull my list from my bag and do some more research.

Hours passed before I even realized it was dark outside. I was so consumed by my research videos, I'd even missed cat feeding time, and Minion hadn't noticed, either. She was too busy sleeping, curled up next to me, her tiny paw on my foot. Looking at my fitness tracker watch, I saw it was after nine, so I lazily got up, earning more judgment and dirty looks from Minion until she heard me open the cabinet. She came running, tail up and happy. I laughed and set her full bowl down. Then I started thinking about what I was going to eat. It was so late, though, and I was going to bed, so I decided not to eat anything more than a bowl of cereal. I turned off the TV and went to bed. Five a.m. came early.

Monday again. I could never understand why people hated Mondays so much. I hated Tuesdays because they moved slower than molasses in a Pennsylvania January. Mondays moved so fast, I never really knew the difference between the start of the workday and the end. I liked it that way. On occasion, I did like to kick back and relax, and rewarded myself with Tuesday off since I'd gotten everything handled on Monday and Julie could run the place blindfolded. Maybe I'd try that again one day—payback for the spider joke.

Tuesday, I woke up and jogged and showered. The weather was less than stellar, feeling sticky and soupy and suffocating. Even Minion felt it, bathing every ten minutes. I set the air conditioner to seventy as soon as I got home from my jog, but after my warm shower, it didn't help much. I turned on every ceiling fan in the house just to get the air moving and my skin feeling better. I hated getting out of the shower and immediately sweating again, but these things happened in Florida, so I resigned myself to another shower before bed. Between now and then, however, I still had a few more hours of research.

I finally had everything I needed for Alex. I was bummed I couldn't do anything else hobby related, but I also, undoubtedly, didn't want to out myself. I'm a serial killer. I'm not a vigilante type or anything like that. And I'm no Ed Gein, Jeffrey Dahmer, or Aileen Wuornos My fuck! If I was a professional lot lizard killing truck drivers, I'd be a fucking moron.

She got away with it for a while, too. So did the rest.. Unlike those losers, I was gifted. And I intend to never get caught.

I watched documentaries about BTK, Dahmer, Gein, all of the worst. Hell, I even took notes from fictional serial killers. Unlike that psychiatrist, I wasn't a cannibal, and I didn't have a code like that blood spatter guy in Miami.

What I did have was a list of pet peeves, grievances whose violation was torture and death. I used that list and my imagination to conduct my hobby.

Oh, I also had studied police procedural textbooks and crime scene cleanup books more than the CSI guys. I needed every edge I could get.

And I never rushed my kills. Oh no. I carefully plot, sometimes for months—it's painful—to make sure all goes according to plan. I didn't get this far in life without careful, detailed planning. The devil might be in the details, but ask my victims, and they'd say the devil was in me.

Oh wait. That's right. You can't ask them because they're all dead. Because I killed them.

Research and planning were two things I loved, and no source was too obscure. I even took notes on unsolved single murders. Some of those police and coroner reports were really insightful, though I felt like the authorities bungled things or hid a lot. I'm not talking about unsolved from six months ago, I'm talking six years and more in the past. Sometimes I learned things, most times nothing, particularly because I did further research to find out that DNA had been used at some point between then and the present and the killer caught.

As far as I know, the only other one who was never caught was Zodiac. But even he was different from me. He killed for attention. That's not what I do. I kill because I have a need, a dark side that is largely driven by my imagination, and by those who push the limits of my pet peeves. I don't expect I'm making the world a better place; I just kill because getting these assholes out of the way makes my life much easier. And in the final analysis, I'm really all I care about.

Like I said, part of my drive and instinct for self-preservation meant I was a careful researcher. I even took notes on how not to dispose of a body. I wasn't getting caught; I was too young to go to prison. I was sure there would come a day I'd have to leave Florida altogether for a life elsewhere if the cops ever got too close, but for now, I wanted to enjoy it.

I petted Minion and showered again and went to bed with a smile on my face, knowing the day would soon come when I'd get to indulge in my favorite hobby again. I even dreamed that night about some of my past kills, my favorites reel, and awoke feeling rested for the first time since my last hobby time.

I had a natural bounce in my step today, which usually occurred only after hobby time, but I was happy, so I didn't cover it up. I also, somehow, forgot to cover my left arm tattoo—barbed wire from shoulder to wrist with sporadic poppy flowers along the barbed wire. I had two others, though they were fully covered. On my right arm I had death with a woman's face and elegantly dressed like the TV mom Morticia, and on my back, I had a monarch with its wings spread out to cover the majority of my back, its thorax right down my spine. It stopped just at the bottom of my rib cage.

I walked into the office, causing Julie to look up from her desk, the phone up to her ear, giving me a questioning look. I continued to my office, knowing she'd come ask when she was finished writing down messages. She did about two minutes later.

"You know you have a meeting today with the mayor, right?" Condemnation was apparent in her tone.

"I do," I shot back, "and I have a sweater in the closet."

Julie made a face that looked like the emoji with the open eyes and the straight-line mouth and went back to her desk. Julie, my friends, and my father were the only people allowed to speak to me in such tones without receiving threats, verbal or non, as a retort.

Ten

IT WAS FOUR O'CLOCK on Friday, and I was expecting Alex's call any minute, ready to hear how the week had gone. I was also expecting one from Dr. Osten to report Alex's hours and let me know if I needed to find someone else for the position. Surprisingly, Dr. Osten called first with nothing but praise for Alex. He said he'd told Alex to get the blue scrubs at the scrub shop. Even I knew which color meant what. The discussion of the terms of making Alex entirely his employee lasted all of three minutes. We had this down to a science. I knew the types of people the doctor preferred for which positions, so I was also his human resources director to a degree. We wished each other a nice weekend, agreed to celebratory drinks tonight at seven, and hung up.

Julie left just before the phone rang again. This time, it was Alex. I didn't let him know the doctor already called, having wanted him to share his happiness. He was so excited he could barely speak.

I, however, was annoyed yet again by how polite he managed to be, even while excited. He kept apologizing for speaking so fast and thanked me over and over for placing him with Dr. Osten. I lost count of how many apologies and thank yous I'd received before I grew tired of it and professionally ended the call. I placed my fingertips on each temple, rubbing in slow circles. That guy gave me a headache of pure annoyance. I couldn't wait until he was dead by my hand.

I packed up and left, headed for the restaurant where I was to meet Dr. Osten, intending to eat before drinks. As I drove, I chose pop punk to listen to; I think the kids called it emo. It didn't matter, I needed to hear some Panic and Fall Out Boy. Particularly "Don't Threaten Me with a Good Time" and "I Don't Care." They were fun and helped me feel less annoyed and ready to be around people.

The songs also helped me get through the traffic. Fridays usually weren't so bad, but today was such a nice day, it appeared everyone in the country was out and on the roads.

The whole drive, aside from my music, was nothing but weird. At least I felt better, even if my plans were developing at a snail's pace, aggravating me. I knew I had to keep my body count low and slow or risk being caught, but I was tormented by impatience.

I reached the restaurant right before Dr. Osten arrived. *So much for dinner*. We did choose a table, at my insistence, given I was hungry and needed food. Dr. Osten wouldn't hear of my paying for anything, including my meal, and ordered the most expensive merlot on the list. The man's name fit him, even if it wasn't quite the word it should be.

We caught up while we waited for the wine, him bragging about his daughter getting into the Harvard pre-med program and his oldest, his son, being promoted to major in the Marine Corps with an offer to work in the Pentagon.

I was only half listening.

Osten was pompous but well meaning. He was brought up in a well-to-do family up north, Massachusetts or somewhere like that, so he always came off as snobbish. He really was a good man and a good friend. I considered myself lucky to

have him as a client and friend. Since we met, he'd invited me over to Christmas dinner every year. He even gave me a gift "as a token of his appreciation, thanks, and love for me" almost as if I were his own. That's the part that made me feel a little uncomfortable.

I held myself to, honestly, all but impossible standards and goals. Him telling me that he felt like I was one of his kids should've made me feel like I could do anything, that I was all I'd ever wanted and more, but it accomplished the opposite.

I'd spent my life being told I wasn't good enough and fell into believing it until my father had a change of heart and he and I grew closer the older I got. He encouraged me to try everything I wanted, to be who I wanted to be. So I did. I tried a lot, and I failed a lot. But I kept getting back up.

I'm a fighter, and I wanted nothing more than to succeed at running my own business. My father's definition of success varied from mine, but we both agreed I was successful and happy, which was all that mattered to him. Yet when I'd hear those things from Osten, I always felt like a fraud under his piercing gaze. I stopped thinking about it the second the waiter showed up with the wine. I'd always allowed what I perceived as other's judgments to make me feel small and fake. My therapist and I were working on that.

"Dear, are you all right? You've barely said a word since we got here," Osten said, cocking his head to the side, eyeing me as though I might have a fever.

"Oh sorry. Yes, yes. I'm all right. Lost in my own thoughts again," I laughed.

I turned to the waiter and ordered the grilled chicken with mashed potatoes and broccoli. Osten ordered the same. It was only now, after many years of knowing him, that I actually took in what I was looking at. He was a balding forty-eight-year-old man, portly but not overweight, a hair under six feet tall, with very pronounced features, and those eyes. They were beady like a rat but blue.

He wasn't awful to look at, but he wouldn't ever be in a bed with me. I'd much rather gnaw my own arm off. As I was vividly imagining myself doing just that, Osten launched into how perfect a fit Alex was for his office.

I perked up. My impatience to kill the guy grew as I listened to Osten talk about how polite he was and punctual and everything we both valued in an employee. Was I the only one who saw *how* polite Alex was made him like a fucking gnat!

"Yes, he's very polite. I'm glad I sent him to you. Will you have him still handling the billing and insurance?" I needed to know how much Alex would be missed by Osten, and I knew damn well I couldn't take out the most prominent plastic surgeon in the tri-county area.

"He will." Osten sipped and nodded. "More on the insurance side, as I'd like to take on more reconstruction surgeries. I'm sick of all the saline and collagen and other *fillers*. I want more meaning in my career. Don't get me wrong, the desire to be physically perfect has made me a renowned physician, but it's grown cold."

I'll give you something else cold—Alex's body on ice. The waiter returned as I sipped my wine, smiling at Osten as he thanked me again for helping him. Our plates were set down in front of us, and we clinked glasses to another great employee and continued successful relationship. We ate and talked aimlessly about Passing Through, and I couldn't help gushing about Julie and how perfect she was to eventually take the wheel of the company for me so I could travel and check more things off my bucket list, most of which were murder related. While we talked, I was busy plotting how to make Alex suddenly look unreliable and incompetent. It would take time, but I'd learn to control my need.

Eleven

On the way home, all I could think was how I was going to destroy Alex so I could kill him without him being missed. Osten loved the guy, which was great but also terrible. Maybe I should've sent him elsewhere so this wouldn't be an issue. Duly noted and tucked away for future reference. After our meal, we finished the bottle, toasting again to a continuously fruitful relationship. Osten even had valet pull my Jeep up before his BMW because he was still a gentleman. We parted ways with him telling me he'd have me over soon for a cookout and cocktails. That meant catered barbecue and a professional bartender—er, mixologist—or whatever they called themselves these days.

I drove home mulling over the fact that before I knocked off my intended target, I was going to destroy his career so almost no one would know he was missing. I'm not a psychopath nor am I a sociopath. I know right from wrong, and I have empathy. I know it's wrong to kill, but I still do it. I like it, and it makes me feel good.

I won't divulge how many I've already taken down, but know I've earned the title of serial killer. The FBI defined serial murder as "the unlawful killing of two or more victims by the same offender(s), in separate events." That fit. For around three years, I've been an active killer with a few more than two dead. So, I've got on-the-job experience

My last was only about a month or so ago, and I like large-gaps between, so the cops don't suspect anything. I don't even kill them the same way. One guy got an ax through the back of his skull for cutting an elderly lady off in line at the grocery store. So, I followed him and learned his daily patterns and habits, and...Anyway, I'm not a typical serial killer.

When I got home, it was close to ten. I wasn't really tired, so I fed Minion and took a shower, and we cuddled in bed watching a streaming show based on a book about an abused woman and her group of friends who are all in on a lie about how her husband died. I got so into the show, I didn't realize the time until the end of the first season. I looked at the alarm clock, and the red lights read seven a.m. It was time to go for my jog and get ready for—today was Saturday. I could go to sleep for a few hours. I had no plans.

I opened my eyes and rolled over to a blurry 12:01 p.m. Minion was happily drooling and purring, staring at me with big sleepy eyes that kept closing. So did mine, though I couldn't help but think we should, at least, get out of bed.

"Come on, M, we have to get out of bed." I reached over to pet her, glazed eyes begging me not to leave the warm comfort.

Then I thought about it. What did I really *have* to get done today? Nothing that couldn't be procrastinated until tomorrow. I could take a day off jogging and plotting.

Besides, I hadn't really come up with anything yet, other than to somehow make Alex's bus late. He did say he always preferred to take the bus unless he absolutely had to drive. It was cheaper and easier for him. I respected that the guy knew his personal life so well. So did I, which is why I had to firmly put those boundaries about him coming to my house to leave flowers in a no-fly zone. But he wasn't my employee anymore. Could I really make people believe we were having an affair under the pretenses of offering to "mentor" him or maybe break from those boundaries and give the guy a "friend"?

M stood up and stretched, pulling my mind from what could have been the beginning of some mean girl's plot in high school because she wasn't treated properly at home and got no attention, so if she had to ruin someone's formative years, so be it. Hell, that's what helped shape adult me. I was bullied for being taller than most girls, and I was kind of nerdy. I got good grades, went to college on partial academic scholarship, but there were others who were part of the "in" crowd, smarter, with full rides to Yale and Oxford. Of course, *those* girls were never bullied like me. It sucked, but I trudged my way through and became the successful woman I am now.

Some would say I killed because of how I was treated in high school. Multiple psychiatrists have found that I had a very "normal" experience, that it didn't make me hate the world or want retribution or anything stupid like that. In fact, they called me "well adjusted." At least I had that going for me—without having manipulated them, no less.

M curled up in my hair, purring, drooling, and kneading at my face. I wasn't getting out of bed anytime soon. If having a cat had taught me only one thing, it was if they're comfortable, leave them be, even if you have to go to the

bathroom. Cats sure had a way to make you feel guilt like humans couldn't—you will be judged harshly for failing to keep them comfortable, and they will make you feel like you kicked them while walking down the hall. I supposed it was because they're defenseless against humans, but one look into those big pleading eyes, and my heart melted every time. My eyes closed.

Darkness filled the room, and I wondered if it was a dream. Shaking my head and sitting up, I couldn't see Minion sleeping, though I felt her next to my calf. The clock was blinking 3:47. I'd lost three hours and forty-seven minutes to a power outage. *Great*. I pulled my phone from the nightstand and prepared for the onslaught of light. Six-thirty a.m. on Sunday. I'd managed to sleep Saturday away with almost zero planning to make Alex irrelevant.

Minion stirred, instinctively knowing what time it was. We stretched and went downstairs, her sounding more like a giant cat than the tiny thing she was. I fed her and went back upstairs to get ready for my jog. Looking out the bedroom window as I brushed my teeth, I noted the day was a perfect day for planning—dreary and dark, just like my current mindset. The thoughts of a whispered "affair" with Alex came rushing back. I smiled.

Twelve

MONDAY CAME AROUND LIKE always, with me in a cheerful mood having set things in motion. Alex was none the wiser; at the moment; neither was anyone else. Julie greeted me, though she seemed down, and I don't think it was the weather. Not that I knew her well enough yet to know if gloom affected her that way or not. I set my bag down and hung my coat in my office before walking back out to Julie. I felt a chill in the air as I walked away from the coat rack, causing the hair on the back of my neck to stand up. *What the fuck?* Apparently, Julie felt it too. We ran into each other as I started to walk out of my office.

"Yikes! Sorry." Julie blushed.

"No worries." I smiled.

"Did you just feel that? It made the hair on the back of my neck stand up." She was visibly shaking.

"I did and was coming to see if you did, too. I'll check the air conditioner setting; maybe it's off or something. Also, I couldn't help but notice you looked a little down when I walked in. Are you okay?"

"Yeah, I guess. It's no big thing."

I didn't believe her. "I hope you know you can talk to me about anything." I hugged her and walked to the thermostat.

It was one of those fancy, high-tech things you have to be taught how to use if you're not a tech geek, which neither of us was.

"Awesome," I sighed, "we'll have to call the AC company. The panel is doing something weird. Must be from Sunday morning's power flash."

"I'll get right on it." Julie jogged to her chair, rolled to the phone, and started dialing.

Back in my office, I heard Julie shrieking at the poor receptionist of the AC company, something about two hours was unacceptable. I had to intervene, or she may have ripped out the throat of the person she was talking to on the phone I used that messaging service we had in the office to communicate, particularly when I was interviewing or one of us was on the phone. I typed "Julie, two hours is fine. Breathe.' She responded with "K." That was jarring. She'd never K'd me. Something was definitely wrong. I decided that once the AC repair people left, she and I were having a girls' day and closing the office.

Right before I paid the bill, I told Julie to set the voice mail and grab her things. She scrunched up her face but did as I asked. Turns out, we needed a new panel; the power flare had fried the one we had. That would be another two-hour wait for another day. I scheduled with the AC guy, he left, and we weren't far behind.

I motioned for Julie to get in the passenger side of the Jeep, and she did. I jumped in, backed out, smirked like we were teenagers sneaking out after curfew, and took off. Julie laughed, catching on, though not fully. She had no idea what was going on or where we were off to, but she was more than happy to be along for the ride.

"How was your meetup this weekend?" I asked her.

Julie sighed heavily. "I don't really want to talk about it."

"So that's why you're as gloomy as the weather. Well, nothing like a girls' day of shopping to get you out of your funk!"

"Brit, I'm cheap. Like dollar-store and thrift-store cheap; you know this. I'm trying to buy a house and a new car. That Camry is, like, ten years old, no matter how good it looks. The maintenance is getting more expensive. I hate having payments, but I want an upgrade."

I raised my brows a few times, inquiring about a Jeep. Julie laughed. "No, I don't want a Jeep. These get expensive, and I see how quickly obsessed you grew. I don't want that."

"Okay, okay. I get it. Any idea what you'll replace the Camry with?"

"I was test-driving some SUVs, and I really like the Acura MDX and the Kia Sorento. The Sorento is half the price tag with almost all the same features. The MDX has things I'd never use and really don't want to spend fifty-four thousand on. I think I'm going with the Sorento."

I nodded my approval. Not that Julie needed it; she'd buy whatever vehicle she wanted. I think she just liked having it.

We pulled under the parking garage to a ground-level parking spot in front of Macy's. Westshore Plaza held a special place in my heart. It was one of the few malls left and one of the fewer I actually liked. We walked through to Irish 31 and sat at the bar. The mixologist asked if we were ready to order, and I ordered a round of afternoon delights for us, putting a fifty-dollar bill on the counter.

He was cute and had dark hair, blue eyes, and nice smile. Julie was checking him out, too. She blushed a bit when he turned to look at her, causing them both to smile and put their heads down.

Julie suddenly scowled. I put my hand on her back to comfort her, but she gently pushed me away.

"Okay, spill."

"Not until we have our drinks. That bartender is cute, but I want our conversation to be as private as can be in a bar."

I nodded my acceptance. I understood the pains of dating, which was part of why I had stopped. When you have such high expectations for yourself, others can easily cause you to feel down about yourself because they're not the one you imagined to be your perfect fit.

Since then, I'd learned to take others in stride and kind of compartmentalize how high my self-expectations were from my friends and even my father. I loved him; don't misunderstand. He was my father, and I wasn't keen to share my reasons for being so good at compartmentalizing at this point, which was good for me since he won't ever get married again. After all, the woman had given birth to the wonder that was me.

I wanted to try to teach Julie how to compartmentalize, but that's not who she was, and I never wanted her to change for me or anyone else. She was a sweet girl, and I loved her like I did my friends. I'd never intentionally corrupt any of them. That's why none knew my secrets.

The cutie came back and gave us our drinks. Instead of taking the fifty, he started a tab, knowing that fifty-dollar bill was going places. He smiled at Julie as he said he hoped we enjoyed our drinks and if we needed anything else, his name was Cody.

Okay, Cody, you're on. Julie here thinks you're hot and wants to fuck your brains out. Maybe more than once if she likes it.

I giggled, and Julie turned to me, raising her glass. "To the best boss a girl could ever hope for. Brit, you're smart, beautiful, kind, encouraging, make me feel empowered at work and my personal life...I could go on all day, but I simply want to say thank you. Thank you for choosing me out of the many you interviewed and thank you for your tutelage and friendship." She wiped a tear from her eye with her free hand, and so did I.

"To the best everything I could ever hope for and for choosing, above all the other job offers you received, to come with me because you believe in us as a team and our unexpected friendship." We clinked and sipped. This cocktail was delicious and destructive. Mental note: no more than three of these—ever.

Julie set her drink down and told me all about her MatchMe meetup. The poor thing. I'd have sworn off dating after that, but she wanted more from life, and I respected that.

I once had too, but she truly deserved all the happiness in the world, even if it was something as simple as a silly little smiley face sticker that made her feel that way. But this guy, man, I wanted to kill him in Alex's stead, though that was already in careful planning and too late to deviate from.

Turned out Julie's date arrived half an hour late, then got drunk at the restaurant, then verbally abused her. When someone tried to stop him, he drunkenly swung at them. Julie took an Uber home, crying all the way, thinking something was wrong with her. This was the type of guy she attracted and why she attempted to date twice a year. I hugged her as she wiped away another tear.

"There is absolutely *nothing* wrong with you. You're perfect the way you are, and you'll find someone who agrees with me," I said as we hugged.

Neither of us noticed Cody eavesdropping and were startled when he came back to check on us.

Thirteen

"HOW IS EVERYTHING, LADIES?" Cody queried. A shocked and wide-eyed Julie couldn't do anything but stammer. I nodded and raised my glass to him, a sign that we were fine and please make another round. He nodded in acknowledgment and started off to make more. Julie sipped her drink and shook the shock away.

"That was creepy." She quivered. "How much do you think he heard?"

"Enough, I'm sure." I sipped. "But now he probably knows you needed the day off and a few drinks and some food. By the way, I've never been here, so I can't recommend anything to eat."

As I finished my sentence and we laughed, Cody came back with our second round. "I can. The bangers and boxty is amazing! Would you like me to put an order in for you, ladies?"

We looked at each other, Julie's eyes telling me how creepy he was again and that whatever I ordered was fine with her as long as it wasn't squid.

"We'll take two then please, Cody." I smiled. He turned around to put the order in the computer.

I leaned into Julie, whispering. "Okay, so he's been creepy twice, but the second time he was a lot more awkward than the first. Just try to hold a conversation with him. Maybe get his number and text him on your terms."

Julie nodded. She smiled as I pulled away to sip my freshly made drink.

I wanted to test the guy myself before letting her anywhere with him, but getting them to talk seemed less parental than grilling him. He turned back from the computer to apologize for seeming creepy, and he and Julie struck up an honest conversation. He told her he bartended and took classes for engineering at USF. He grew up in Tampa and was interested in engineering because he wanted to help design a new and better drainage system.

That was commendable, given half the city floods when it rains hard, which is almost every summer day. Julie told him I was her boss and friend, and they gabbed the time away until our food arrived. He let us eat in peace, only asking our thoughts when he came to take the empty plates. He even brought a third round of cocktails. He was either very good at his job or trying hard to impress us. I left it at both.

Before we left to go shopping, Julie got his number as I paid, tipping him handsomely. As we walked out, I turned my head just enough to see the shock on his face at his payment for a job well done. Julie was happy, I was happy, and we'd just had the best lunches after months of half-crappy take-out.

Julie had a skip in her step now, and all I could do was smile. We were both grateful for each other, and a spontaneous girls' day out to help her feel better worked considerably more than I'd planned.

We went into numerous stores, trying on things we liked and even things we didn't, having our own montage of terrible outfits. I paid for everything—I'd earned it, and Julie quickly learned not to fight me on it. I told her to think of the clothes as gifts—gifts of my appreciation for her—if that helped, and on our way out, I asked her how comfortable she felt running the office when I wasn't in.

She said very.

Then I asked her how she'd feel interviewing applicants.

She stopped in her tracks as I held the door open.

"Wait, are you retiring already?" She squealed in panic.

"No," I laughed and hooked her arm in mine. "I'm just wordering what your plans for the future are and if, maybe one day, you'd like to be the one in my office running the show.'

We got to my Jeep, put the bags in the back, and hopped in.

Julie was silent until I started it up. "I think I'd like that. One day. Not now. I'm not ready for all that responsibility."

I loved this girl. Not only the best possible hiring decision I'd ever made but honest, too. One day we'd be thick as thieves.

I pulled out of the spot and got back on the 275 toward the office. As I dropped Julie at her car, she lunged at me as I helped put her bags in, crushing my windpipe in a bear hug.

"Thank you. For today, for everything!"

I couldn't respond other than to tap her shoulder so she might realize she was choking me. She did and quickly loosened up.

"You're welcome. Now go home, and I'll see you in the morning."

We parted ways, and I imagined her hearing from Cody as soon as he finished work, which turned out to be true when Julie came in glowing the next morning. Apparently, they'd been on the phone all night and he was "so smart and funny and caring." Inside, I wanted to vomit; outside, I showed the happiness I genuinely felt for her. She needed more than her cat, and I hoped Cody might be that something.

She'd mentioned they were going to the movies, not as a date or anything, but to see if they might be further compatible. Julie had gotten smart about guys overnight. Then she told me it was his suggestion, to help her see that he wasn't the kind of asshole she usually attracted.

I thought that was sweet and vowed to do my due diligence and look into him, including call my contacts in the police department. Julie wouldn't know unless the guy had a bad past.

We went about our day as usual, only I conducted research on Cody. I'd had all I needed, for now, about Alex, and I enjoyed searching people's pasts.

Cody came up clean. He came from a good family, a decent neighborhood, got good grades growing up and in his college career. There was nothing out of place with him. Suffice it to say, I wasn't suspicious. He'd given me no reason to be.

The day went on with nothing unusual or notable happening. Julie and I made pencil plans for another dinner soon and each went home.

Although the sun was setting, I decided to jog again when I got home. Something wasn't sitting right in my thoughts, and jogging helped me process. I didn't take my usual route up Bayshore but through the neighborhoods, ending up in front of Alex's building. I didn't bother to question why; I knew why.

I wanted to murder him, but it wasn't the time. The thoughts that didn't sit right were those of impatience. I wanted the cops to remain clueless from last month. I'd left nothing at that scene, or any other, that could tie them together, let alone to me.

Out of my peripheral vision on the left, I saw someone walking. It was Alex. I looked both ways and jogged across the street to meet him at his door. I startled him so fully, he fell backward, tripped, and landed on his tailbone.

"Oh! Are you all right?" I bent down to help him up, internally laughing hysterically.

"I, uh, what, I—" He took the offered hand and stood back up. "What are you doing here? Didn't you say this was inappropriate?"

"Well, you happen to be along one of my jogging routes, but yes, I did say that. What if I wanted to take it back?" I lured him with big eyes and a devilish smile.

He was taken aback and scratched the back of his head. "Can I think about it?"

WHAT! Think about it? That come get me *look gets everyone. How can you not say yes?*

"Sure. Sorry I scared you." Feeling awkward and unable to think of a witty retort, I just smiled at him as I put my earbuds back in and jogged back home. This was going to be more difficult than I first thought. I had felt sure Alex would jump at my blatant invitation. Hmm. Bring it on, Alex.

Fourteen

JOGGING HOME, I DEVIATED course three times, taking a route three times longer than my usual. I was agitated and even mad and a little put off by him asking to think about it. No one, I mean *no one*, turned me down, sweaty or not. And my looks were merely the icing on the cake. People loved my personality, that I was always willing to help out and do any-thing I could for those close to me and even strangers. I put Alex in my number-one-client-slash-closest-thing-to-a-sec-ond-family's office, knowing I was going to kill him. I had done it because he showed a lot of potential. I'd never make that mistake again. I borderline thought he was being un-grateful; then I came to the conclusion he was protecting himself. I'd already threatened him if he broke the bound-aries I set. But I was the one breaking them; that had to count for something.

Then, I'd thought he'd probably never been with a woman, and if he had, it was only a kiss. What didn't occur to me until I'd gotten home was that he was rather experienced, just kept it to himself. Almost like he didn't want to flaunt it. I laughed, moving on with my evening.

By the time I'd gone to bed, I'd run through every possible scenario of how the accidental meeting with Alex could've gone. It was truly accidental. I'd had no plans to jog near his apartment, let alone bump into him. I was simply jogging out my frustration at not being able to kill him then.

Maybe I was missing something about him because every scene ended with him falling all over himself like the day he'd first walked into my office. What had changed? Maybe there was a girl in Osten's office he had a crush on? I decided to call Osten in the morning. He always knew what was going on in his office.

The best part is his employees think him none the wiser. That was only part of why I enjoyed the man so much. He really did look out for me after we first met. In fact, he'd asked me if I knew anyone in any of my classes looking to temp for him, leading me into Passing Through after all the other failures during college. Osten was one of my biggest fans, second only to my birth father.

They'd met once or twice and adored each other. Osten loved how blunt my father is, and my father loved that Osten was a good influence in my life.

If I ever got caught, it would kill the two of them. So, I vowed to never get caught. My mind wandered off to thoughts of a book I'd just picked up about little known serial killers, and I fell asleep, Minion curled next to my stomach.

Every day brought more of the same: more Julie gushing about Cody, more temps to interview, which I had Julie sit in on a few so she could feel comfortable conducting them if I took a day off. And more Alex ignoring me.

Osten agreed to listen to the office whispers and kept me updated weekly, but nothing fluttered that held weight. Alex had been there a little over a month now, not including the week he worked for me, and was very friendly with his coworkers but nothing signaling an office romance. It was disconcerting.

I understood not wanting an office romance. Hell, I'd had office one-night stands and friends with benefits. They always got attached, though. Even after I'd made it impenetrably clear I wanted nothing other than sex, as I was too focused on my career.

What was it with men and confident women? I had girl crushes on confident women, but I didn't claim to be in love with them, unless they've really done some amazing things. Besides, that's a different kind of love. It's not romantic love; it's adoration and admiration.

I was at a dead end of sorts on what to do next. I had a lot of thinking ahead of me, a lot more planning. This Alex guy was frustrating as fuck, and it made me less than happy. I'll admit I'd been in a less-than-stellar mood about it but was making my way out.

I hated that someone could have that much power over me, and I worked hard to change it, vowing to keep it that way from this point on. I pushed forward with different plans for Alex's downfall. If none of them worked, a simple kidnapping would have to do.

Osten wasn't the type to get the cops involved if one of his employees never came back. Good for me, right? Sure, he'd ask me questions, wondering if I'd heard from him, but lies were second nature for me.

I found myself buried under a rather literal mountain of paperwork, neglected due to my obsession with being turned down. I started staying late or taking work home with me to get it all finished. Even Julie was surprised how much I'd let go. I promised her it would never happen again.

"Hey, Brit!" Julie called into my office one Friday night after I'd dug myself out.

"What's up?"

"Let's go for drinks, just me and you. We haven't been able to talk because you've been so busy, and I miss us." She sounded disheartened.

I was silent for a moment, having just been smacked in the face with guilt.

"Yeah, where to?"

"There's that new karaoke place on Fletcher." She pepped up. "I've been wanting to go since it opened."

"You are not getting me to sing," I laughed.

"We'll see." Her smirk was audible.

We decided to take an Uber, particularly because I needed a well of alcohol after letting my self-esteem take such a big and being so behind on paperwork.

Walking into this karaoke place was a whole new experience for me. I'd never been to karaoke before, only seen videos of others doing it. It was loud, and I was almost positive someone was murdering a cat in there somewhere. The awful generic version of whatever that garbage parading as music was combined with the voices of the three on stage, creating a cacophony I thought would make my eardrums rupture. I shielded my ears, allowing Julie to lead me to the bar, then to a table.

I looked at Julie and mimed asking how we expected to have a conversation. Julie laughed at my horrific attempt at charades and sipped her drink. I decided to down mine and start a tab. This night wasn't going to end well, and I wanted to be as prepared as I could for praying to the porcelain gods if my body chose that route.

The music stopped between singers but not long enough for a real conversation. I wanted to know all about how Julie was doing and what was going on in her world.

I really didn't have much to talk about since I'd shut everyone and everything out for over a week because of a hiccup in my plans. I had mulled over making it a torturous, slow death or a quick and painless one. In the end, no matter how I prepared, it always came down to my mood at killing time. I snapped myself out of my murderous reverie and focused on my friend.

Julie got up to sing a Britney Spears song, and I felt obligated to join her, given my mother had such an affinity for her—that's how I was named. We decided "Work, Bitch" wasn't what we wanted and chose "Lucky," largely because my name is Britney and everyone who meets me thinks I'm lucky, when all I do, in truth, is work hard. Yes, everything was always all about me.

We sang and danced and, of course, received a standing ovation. We had to steady ourselves on each other when we bowed because we almost fell over. Waving, we stepped down from the stage to the manager running up to us clapping, a blinding smile on his face. He asked us if we'd consider coming back two or three nights a week to help him draw people in. He even offered to pay us.

I laughed. Julie did, too. Then I realized he was every bit as serious as I was about killing Alex. We asked if we could take the weekend to think about it, and he happily agreed. Apparently, while we sang our drunken hearts out, quite a few people had come in from watching someone's live video of us on social media. I did feel like a celebrity in the moments of trying to pay our tab and being told our drinks were covered—by everyone from the house to some other patrons. We teased our way out, telling those asking when we'd be back to call the bar to find out.

Julie somehow managed to request and get us the same Uber driver we had on the way here. She was happy to see us and yelled at me for the tip I left on our first trip, so she comped us the second trip. Then I told her we'd need her again if she was still working. She said she'd stay on just for us because she liked us. We got to getting to know her. She was twenty-five, in college, no kids or boyfriend, and her name was Nicole. I liked her a lot, and so did Julie. We exchanged numbers so she could let us know when she was working if we needed her.

We had her take us to another bar on North Dale Mabry so we could eat and talk and keep drinking. I invited her to join us, at least to eat, but she had another fare waiting.

We agreed another time would be best, and Julie and I walked inside, choosing to sit at the bar. We switched over to mojitos, which were buy-one-get-one, and looked at the half-price apps menu. We decided on the pretzels with beer cheese, wing bites, and nachos. The carbs would soak up the alcohol, so that was either a good thing or bad, depending on how you chose to look at it.

Once our drinks were served, Julie launched into a breathless monologue about Cody and how he was everything she'd hoped him to be. She even got into the sticky details, making me lurch more than once.

I patted her arm, signaling I really didn't need to know such information, but she kept talking.

She finally stopped when the food arrived about ten minutes later. She took a deep breath, downed her mojito, turned to me with her tomato-red face, and smiled.

"Sounds like you're really happy," I joked.

Julie laughed and dug into the nachos. I was glad for her silence and the sounds around us. It'd been a while since I heard someone say so much in such a short time.

While we ate and drank, I thought of other ways I could get to Alex. If Osten wasn't hearing anything around the office, I had to figure out another way.

Kidnapping was the last option. *Alex, my dear, bumbling, polite Alex. What have you done?*

Fifteen

SURPRISINGLY, I HAD NO signs of a hangover the following day. I woke early, too, so I decided to jog my Bayshore route twice. Somehow, I had what felt like limitless energy until I got home and took a shower. Then the headache from hell started. I took some Tylenol and picked up some of the books I'd borrowed from the library about serial killers. Most had broken into homes or kidnapped people. Except Gein. Between that guy and H.H. Holmes, their houses must've stunk to the point of projectile vomiting. I almost did just reading about the things they did and the things they kept so they didn't get caught. Keeping a dead body in my house is not the kind of disposal I preferred. Some I'd fed to gators in Alligator Alley; some I'd throw in the barren swamplands. I had always wanted to use a mulcher and some other fancy toys. Maybe even chum for sharks.

With so many options, why did some real and fictional serial killers leave things behind? The only one never caught was Zodiac. It was rumored he was still out among the population today, and if he were, of course I'd want to talk to him.

He'd left a trail of bodies in his wake, played games with the cops, even licked the envelopes and stamps when he sent letters. I started to research if there was a way to identify him, but we're going back over fifty years ago, so nothing he had done, nothing he'd supposedly left would work in my favor. Regardless, I was still interested to know, so I kept looking. No identification was ever made except a partial, and that ruled out someone the cops suspected for a long time.

I felt like I needed to know how he did it, then realized I've gotten away with it and would continue, so why bother worrying about decades-old cases that couldn't be solved? I've never left DNA or anything else to identify me. Shit, I made most of my kills completely and totally unidentifiable. Not even with dental records. Not only did the cops have no idea who I was; they had no clue about the identities of my victims, either.

My phone dinged, pulling me from my thoughts and reading. It was Julie. She'd spent her morning ralphing and drinking water. I looked at the time stamp on the text and the clock on the wall. Shit! Almost three! Where had the time gone? At least I was keeping busy.

I texted Julie back, telling her if she needed anything to let me know, and I'd head over. She thanked me, saying Cody was already on his way. I set my phone down, smiling at her happiness, and before getting back to work, I ran to the kitchen to cut up an apple, adding some salt to the pieces.

Back on the couch, I found myself starting to hunch over, so I took the book I was reading to the table. I spent three more hours going back and forth between the table and couch, reading and soaking in what I could. I retched a few times throughout, still thinking of the stench of decay and rot of Gein's house when he was arrested.

The sun was low, showing a spectacular sky. I did what anyone else would do and went outside to gawk and take photos for Instagram. Nature was truly beautiful, and even a cold-blooded killer could take time to appreciate it.

I appreciated all of nature, from floods to wildfires. Those disasters had reasons for existing, and those reasons were to cleanse and rebuild. Sure, they were tragic, but they were also magnificent beauties only nature could create or keep moving along as nature saw fit. People never liked when I was honest with them about how I saw these things, so I kept those thoughts between myself and close friends who wouldn't belittle me for "wrongthink." I also felt the same about climate change, though that was a cyclical event that the Earth conducted every so often in its own effort to cleanse itself and rebuild. There had been an ice age almost two and a half million years ago; there could be another sneaking up on us. Though that hardly seemed the case now.

No, now was a flooding of the Earth, and no one alive today would be alive then to see the magnificent destruction and beauty that always followed.

Satisfied at my realistic sense of myself and the world, I went back inside to decide on dinner. I called the Uber driver, Nicole, to see if she was working. Not surprisingly, she was. At least they were smart about not drinking and driving.

I picked up my phone and called the Chinese place down the road. I didn't have to say anything—my order was always the same. When the delivery guy showed, he joked about this becoming an every Saturday night thing. I laughed, paid him, and took my food.

Minion was under my feet as I walked into the kitchen. She even went so far as to hop up on the table when I set the food down. I petted her and picked her up, setting her down on the floor while I took her food container out. Minion fed, I could, maybe, eat in peace.

I ate in almost perfect silence, the only sounds being Minion chewing, crickets, and a few birds. This was the most peaceful dinner I'd had in a while and decided to keep that peace going by taking a nice, long, eucalyptus-and-mint bath.

I took my bath complete with a book and a bottle of wine. It was nice to live a life like mine that afforded a master bathroom with a tub I could fit my whole body into without my boobs sticking out or having to bend my knees. I wasn't a bragger, and I never meant to make others feel bad about what I'd accomplished in such a short time. I worked hard, but I worked harder to keep my pride in check.

Taking myself away from my thoughts of work, I dove into the Hemingway book I'd been reading. I'd been trying to finish this book since the day I picked it up and started reading it. Yet, I was always distracted, mostly by my own thoughts. That's how my brain worked, but I was determined to finish this masterpiece of misogyny and darkness. Hemingway himself had demons, not like my love for the kill, but he basically drank himself to death. Regardless, the man's writing was beautiful in a way most couldn't understand, despite his obvious misogyny.

My phone started ringing, pulling me from my book. The caller ID came up with Unknown, so I silenced it, waiting for it to go to voice mail. Then I checked my settings to make sure my phone automatically blocked such calls. It was set to do so. *Hmm, weird.*

As I set the phone back down, the voice mail chimed. I tapped the icon and played it on speaker. It was Alex. He said that's how he got his phone set up—instead of his name, it was Unknown, and he used it to play jokes on his friends. I wasn't sure what friends he was talking about, since I knew he didn't have any. He continued on to say he would text me instead in the future, so he didn't get kicked to voice mail again.

My phone dinged. It was the text Alex said he'd send. opened it and read, "I'm done thinking. I'm sorry. I've decided I'm done with you."

Sixteen

I DROPPED THE PHONE on the floor and went back to reading. Or I tried to. Then I verbally lost my shit. "*You're* done with *me*? Oh, I don't think so, you weasel. I will fucking destroy what you have of a life. Then I will take that life from you. And could you be any more fucking POLITE! I've never met anyone—"

I was cut off by Minion running in, her ears pressed to her head. I'd scared her, and she thought she could save her mommy from harm. How sweet this cat was. I pulled the lever to drain the tub and wrapped myself in a towel as I stepped over the edge. The bathmat was warm and fluffy between my toes. Minion walked up to me, starting to help me dry off by licking the water from my calf, but I pushed her away.

"Baby, that's synthetic crap that can kill you." I kissed her little forehead, petted her, and finished drying off.

I'd thrown on a pair of leggings and a tank top before going back downstairs to keep researching serial killers. One caught my attention after having forgotten about him: Carl Panzram. I didn't recall if I'd ever known he was an arsonist, though this information provided a potential part of the plan. I could set fire to Alex's apartment building, but it was almost one-hundred-year-old original Tampa. It was gorgeous. I'd never been inside, though I did hope whoever renovated the place did so tastefully.

Okay, I'm onto something here. I could mess with one of his appliances and have that set the blaze while Alex isn't home. The real question now was how, precisely, to make it look like an accident. I don't know what's in his apartment, but I'm willing to attempt a peek while he's at work. The research has to be conducted covertly. I suppose I can fiddle with toaster ovens and microwaves and ovens by myself, but where to learn? Oh, Alex, you're a pain in my ass.

I didn't want to use my personal or work laptops and desktop to search for anything, including free used appliances. I wasn't about to make a friend look guilty and use theirs, either.

The only thing left was to somehow get hold of Alex's laptop, and I knew just how to do that. Osten let me anywhere in that office except the surgical suites, which I completely understood. HIPAA and sanitation were huge issues in the medical field these days. I only needed access to the locker room and to know which locker was Alex's.

Osten happily greeted me when I walked into reception. We hugged, and the girls behind the desk excitedly waved to me while they talked to patients on their headsets. Osten walked me to his office, asking what I needed. I told him. I didn't tell him why, and he didn't ask. He gave me the locker number and combination code, making me promise to have one of the girls up front call for him before I left. I promised, kissed his cheek, and set off for the locker room.

It was nine a.m., and everyone was at their desks, so I'd have no interference. If I did, there were bathrooms at the end and on either side of the locker room. The pictures on the wall signifying which side was which had males to the left, females to the right. I guess Osten hadn't caught up with the times yet. Then again, I was too busy looking for Alex's locker, so I didn't notice the third bathroom, newly constructed, with a unicorn on the sign. I guessed that was Osten's way of saying anyone could use it and feel safe. I wanted to know more about it, so I made a mental note to ask Osten before I left.

I finally found Alex's locker in the fourth row on the right-side aisle. Each row was lined with lockers, though they didn't face each other, with benches in the middle. Everyone had ample room to change if they wanted to. I walked down the aisle, finding the proper locker on the bottom of the right side. I used the code and took Alex's laptop out. I sat on the bench and opened the laptop, paying attention for any noise. I opened the browser next, going straight to YouTube. With safe search off, I started typing in things like "How to make a toaster oven look faulty." So what if Alex's insurance company didn't cover his things? Everyone else it affected would be taken care of. I did realized, then, that I needed to make sure everyone was out of the building when I decided to do this. My intent was to destroy, then kill, Alex. No one else needed to get hurt.

I had a hard time finding anything other than how to fix it. I guess I needed the dark web to find such things, which I didn't know how to access. So, I closed everything out and put his laptop back in the bag and his bag back in his locker. I locked it before leaving, hitting the restroom before walking out of the locker room.

Everyone in the office knew me, so no one thought twice about my using the locker room restrooms. A couple of the girls had come in while I was still in my stall. They chattered away, even after locking their stalls. They probably had no clue I was even in here, and neither said a word when the toilet automatically flushed. I washed and dried my hands and left the locker room feeling somewhat defeated. My search, though, wasn't entirely useless. I'd found a lot of videos about repairing wires. Those gave me the knowledge I needed.

I swung by Osten's office, chatting a little before hugging him. "Thank you."

"Any time. Oh! Expect an invitation in the mail this week for the barbecue. It's in three weeks, April something, I can't remember. I expect you'll be there."

"You know it. I'm bringing Julie, as usual."

"Brit, you know I won't remember that, though you do always bring her everywhere…"

"I'm grooming her to take over when I finally decide I want to take up golf," I joked.

Osten laughed and hugged me again. I left, heading directly to Alex's building. I needed to learn if anyone was home right then. My watch read eleven.

Well, I guess I'll have to take days off at random, to figure out when no one's home in the building. It really was a shame I'd be doing this to such an old and beautiful work of architecture.

Seventeen

I STOPPED BY THE office to have lunch with Julie and catch up on anything I missed. Had anything been of real importance, Julie would've called me, and she hadn't. I knew things were in more-than-capable hands. When I walked in, she was on the phone. She gave me that big, sweet grin she has. It was a cross between a goofy grin and a sweet little girl's smile. I don't really have a better way to describe it. She jumped from the desk, nearly crushing me, again, in a bear hug, still talking on her headset. I'd forgotten it was wireless and made a mental note to get one for myself as a just-in-case kind of thing.

Julie pressed the button on the headset, disconnecting the call. I'd been so lost in my own thoughts, I hadn't heard her say goodbye to the person on the other end. She started on a speech of sorts about what had gone on so far that day. It had been busy, and people didn't want to be on hold.

It was mainly those fools who call about ads on job boards instead of following the directions and coming in. I understood people didn't want to waste their time or money on gas or the bus, but if they couldn't follow simple directions, I didn't want them working for my anyhow.

Three people came in, and Julie screened them before having any fill out the paperwork. One passed, so she filled out the paperwork, and Julie scheduled her for an interview the next morning.

"You're sitting in, right?" I asked her.

"I am." Julie blushed.

I put my hand on her shoulder. "You'll be great. I know it Now, let's get some lunch."

Julie took her headset off, set the phones, and grabbed her purse. I locked the door on our way out and drove to a loca place called Moxie's. They had really good sandwiches, anc it'd been too long since I had one. We ordered and sat down.

"So, I'm going to be taking weird days off. Nothing like a vacation, but random."

"Is everything okay?" Julie squeaked as she grabbed my hand.

"I'm fine." I smiled back at her.

That was a flat-out lie. I knew she didn't like being alone much in the office, and I truly felt bad for needing to take a few days off.

I wasn't about to tell her anything that could get her in trouble. I knew the cops would question her during any death investigation of employees, or even previous employ-ees, possibly within hours of finding the body. At least the initial questioning, anyway. Then a more in-depth interview later, if needed. She didn't need to be worried about cover-ing for me and lying. She'd be questioned anyway, having interacted with Alex or anyone else, so the less she knew, the better. Then again, neither of us would be questioned unless Passing Through showed on recent phone records or someone mentioned them working for me or they had no leads. Basically, the cops needed some kind of work relatior or evidence to even think about talking to us.

Our food was delivered by a nice Asian lady, pulling me from my thoughts. I really needed to get a hold on this lost-in-my-own-thoughts thing while in public or around others. They might start thinking I'm losing it. And I'm *definitely* not losing it.

We dug into our sandwiches.

Julie yapped on and on about Cody. She'd even asked him if he had any single friends for me. I spit out my drink at that.

"You didn't have to do that. I don't want a boyfriend, anyway," I told her.

"You may not want one, but you need one." She winked at me.

"You're saying I need to get laid?"

"Well, now that you're laughing so hard, I guess not."

We got up, throwing our trash out as we left, and laughed our way back to my Jeep. The parking lot was a bit of a mess at the moment, but I managed to get out and onto Benjamin. We went back to the office, Julie embarrassed and me still snorting. I'd told her not to feel so bad about it, but she was having a hard time letting it go. Maybe she would after I dropped her off. I made a mental note to call her later and check on her and went to park somewhere and watch Alex's building.

There was a lot more traffic today than I'd expected. Most people were heading back to their jobs from lunch around the same time I dropped Julie off, and it took me almost a half hour to get here after that. I'd found a spot on West Stroud, just beyond the intersection at South Lorenzo, with the driver's side facing the street. I could see all of Alex's building from here. It wasn't a perfectly clear shot, but I was able to see the front door, so I'd see if anyone came in or left.

I was lucky the weather was nice so I could open the windows. I sat watching for hours; so long that I was still there when the three other people who lived in Alex's building came home from work. One observation down. Alex didn't come home for another twelve minutes, walking by me and not even realizing it. *Shit, that was close! I guess I'd need to do some better research next time.*

I was slipping, but Lorenzo only allowed parking on the south side of the road. I wasn't about to earn my own set of cuffs for sitting in the lot of the building across from Alex's. Now I was pissed at myself for not researching the closest bus stop. *What kind of rookie knows their prey takes the bus and doesn't bother to look up the closest stop?* Research on the fly wasn't my strong suit, but it glaringly was an issue I needed to fix.

I sat there until ten p.m. before calling it a night. At least I was mostly successful—learning what time everyone got home was valuable. The next step was to learn when they left. I pulled away from the curb and called Julie to make sure she wasn't still feeling some sort of way about earlier. Her voice sounded chipper, and she said she wasn't, so I let it go at that, and said goodnight.

Eighteen

By Friday, I'd received the invitation to Osten's barbecue. The envelope made it look like a wedding invitation. I opened it, and sure enough, it was about the same kind of thing. The envelope contained the invitation, the RSVP, and the stamped envelope for the RSVP. Osten already knew I was attending and bringing Julie with me. It was rare he invited anyone from his office, so I assumed Alex wouldn't be there. It was set for two weeks from Saturday. I knew it would last into the early hours of the morning—all of Osten's parties did. That was it. That would be the night that I killed Alex.

I'd have to find a suitable place for the act and decide which disposal method I wanted to use. I was thinking to break into the dump and throw him into the hammer mill. That would risk a felony. Not that I wouldn't be anyway. There was a place that let you drive a tank, like a real military tank, and crush cars or just plow through mud. I could plant the body there and let him be destroyed by the tank. *Okay, maybe that's me living out my fantasy to drive a tank, but so what? How cool would it be? And I could be the driver and act terrified and…No, I can't be there when it's found.* There, I had it. I'd drive two hours across the state to dispose of Alex Charles' body.

I was grinning from ear to ear as I filled out the RSVP and dropped it back in my mailbox. Back inside my house, I read and watched how other serial killers killed, as well as recalled my own kills.

I wanted to do something different, something unexpected. Something that a one-time offender would do, maybe. pulled my laptop from its bag and started searching.

I came up with nothing. It appeared no serial killer had ever stabbed a victim in the ear with a pen. *Ha-ha-ha! This is going to be interesting!* The images flowing through my mind were fascinating. They almost made me wish I'd gone to mortuary school. I'd be considered a suspect substantially more than I would be now. The thought of going to observe piqued my interest, though.

I was still in high school when I started killing. But I couldn't think about those times now. I had a victim waiting.

Minion let out a pathetic mew, reminding me it was feeding time. It definitely was, and not just for her. I fed her then went through the pantry to see what I had. There was some organic roasted red pepper soup, and I had cheese bread that just needed to be thrown in the toaster over for a few minutes. I took the tie off the bag of cheese sticks on the counter and laughed at the irony. I was planning to fray the wire to Alex's toaster oven as I used my own. Maybe I was a bit twisted; I had yet to see a psychiatrist who thought otherwise. My parents started taking me back in high school, but that's a story for another time.

While the soup and cheese sticks cooked, I went upstairs to change. As I walked through my bedroom door, I stepped in something cold, wet, and squishy. I lifted my foot to see a furball. *At least I didn't have to be home to hear it.* I was forced to hop my way into the bathroom to clean my foot and grab tissues to clean it up. I had some kind of cat-puke cleaner downstairs, so I changed before cleaning it up. Carefully avoiding the puke, I made my way back downstairs only to grab a rag and the puke cleaner. That was one of the few things in life that grossed me out along with spiders and snakes. As I was cleaning, the microwave and toaster oven beeped and dinged, signaling they were finished. I was, too.

I went back downstairs, thoroughly washed my hands, and took my dinner from both appliances. I sat at the table with a book on serial killers because I couldn't afford to fuck up again.

I finished my dinner then washed and dried the dishes. I took out a bottle of Moscato and a glass and sat back down at the table. Realizing I didn't have a notepad, I got up to grab one so I could sketch out some vague plan. Not in code or anything, not more than two-word bullet points that meant nothing to anyone who would read it. Things like pencils and duct tape. It looked like a shopping list for a home office and other uses—duct tape fixes anything and we all know that. Plus, I Jeep crawl, so I'll always have *at least* one roll in the back at all times.

Now that my serial killer research had been done and body disposal sorted, I needed to figure out when I was setting Alex's apartment on fire. Then I'd offer him the futon until his place was fixed up. I think the real challenge was going to be one of tolerance; how long could I tolerate him and his absurd politeness before I snapped?

I knew I couldn't snap and had to be painfully patient. This was going to make me bitchy, and I hated bitchy me. I liked usual me. I refused to call myself normal because I wasn't and because normal's no fun anyway. I'd get through this. Probably with a lot of wine. Figured I'd be better off stocking up now, since I'd be letting the guy stay here pretty soon.

Monday I went into the office late. I'd left my house around three a.m. and watched Alex's building. Two of the other three residents of that building were professionals and left around seven. The other left shortly after I'd rolled up—I hadn't even shifted into park yet. He looked like a construction worker of some type, and there was always some kind of construction going on around Tampa.

Alex was the last one out of the building, around seven-thirty. I'd looked up the bus route to Osten's office, and it took around forty-five minutes to get there. I'd gotten his schedule from Osten since he'd been moved to deal with the insurance companies. He started at eight a.m., took lunch around one, and clocked out a little after five every day. According to Osten, Alex loved his job and pointing out the insurance company's rules to them. The dude had studied up somehow. I almost didn't want to kill him. Almost.

After Alex passed me, I pulled away, headed for the office. The traffic on North MacDill sucked because it was one lane in either direction, then I hit MLK. Because my office didn't open until nine, and I was late, I was on the lighter side of rush hour, but my route still sucked. I hated tolls or I'd hop on the Vet, but that always backed up, too.

I stopped at the Wawa at Dale Mabry and Waters to grab coffee and donuts. It wasn't unlike me to do things like this, and Julie wouldn't suspect anything weird anyway. What she would call weird would be my offering to let Alex crash at my house until his apartment was renovated. She'd never met him, but after the stunt he pulled with the flowers, she definitely thought the guy was weird and creepy.

I sat in more traffic on the last leg to the office. Taking the donuts and the coffees out of the Jeep was a little complicated, and I assumed the role of magic contortionist to open the door to the office when Julie noticed me staring the door down, trying to figure out what I was going to do. She squeaked as she ran to take something from my hands. Luckily, she grabbed the coffee because we both agreed that spilled coffee was abuse. I sat the donuts on the short wall part of Julie's desk and went into my office to hang my coat and purse before I grabbed one and headed back to my desk. Julie followed with my coffee, talking about someone from Tampa PD calling, wanting to talk to me. She'd written the message down and set it on my desk. I frowned. *What could they possibly need to talk to me about?*

Sighing, I picked up the phone and dialed the number. I reached an Officer Sweet.

"Oh, Ms. Cage. I was hoping you could answer a few questions for me."

Nineteen

"About what?" My heartbeat was no higher than my resting, according to my fitness watch. "Someone reported a prowler over on South Lorenzo around three a.m. They gave us most of a tag number of a Jeep they didn't recognize."

"And that has what to do with me, Officer?"

"What were you doing there?"

"I was making sure a friend got home all right."

"Did you notice anything strange? Maybe someone lurking?"

"You know…I did. As I pulled up, there was a man wearing construction-looking clothes coming out of 1412 South Lorenzo. He was looking all around when he walked away. I didn't think to call because I thought he was just looking to cross the road or something."

"That's very helpful, Ms. Cage. Did you see anything else? Maybe hair color or skin tone?"

"I'm sorry, I didn't. It was too dark, and my windows are tinted."

Sweet let out a sigh. "Okay, well you have my number. If you can think of anything else, please call me."

"I will. Thanks for your call. I don't live too far, so it's nice to be accidentally informed of a prowler." I smiled.

"Well, ma'am, prowlers are generally looking for easy prey, and they don't usually wander too far from home. You live over four miles south. I think you're safe."

"Thanks, Officer. I appreciate the comforting words."

"No problem. Thanks, and have a good day."

"You, too. Be safe." I set the receiver down.

Julie came rushing in, freaking out that something terrible had happened. I told her what the officer wanted, and she asked me why I was there. I told her the same lie I told the officer. I didn't think saying "Oh, I was stalking Alex's apartment so I can break in and mess with his toaster oven to start a fire" would be a good idea.

She calmed down visibly and asked me again if I was okay. I nodded yes and turned to my computer. Now I was bugged that someone was even watching in the first place. This would make the next step substantially more difficult. Maybe I'd ask Alex to borrow his car and set up my Jeep to be worked on for the upcoming rock crawl. I'd take the bus to Alex's, let myself in with his key, fiddle with the wires…Yes this was starting to really come together.

Part of me screamed that I was a blip on the cops' radar; the other part of me shut it down quickly. I was being treated as a witness. That's exactly how I'd be treated if someone saw me leaving Alex's apartment. His car would be gone. I guess people would ask why I didn't use an Uber, which is where I started pointing out the flaws in my own plan.

I'd be treated as a suspect, so I'd have to wait for people to not be around. This would require a full day off and a good hiding place. I'd scoped the street every time I'd jogged it and found a few places to hide out for the day. Or I could pretend I was a gardener at Alex's building. I'd figure it out. Anything to keep my name away from the cops at this point. They got me once, but my lies threw them off.

Could that officer have been so stupid as to *not* ask my friend's name and address? I mean, damn. If this was what was protecting me, I was grateful for my desire to kill.

I spent the rest of the day trying to plot out how I was now going to get into Alex's apartment unnoticed, and the only thing I could think was to somehow be invited in. I suddenly felt like a vampire. I could go knock on his door and offer an apology and do it then. Involving anyone else would be unthinkable. At least, if the nosy neighbor saw me hugging Alex or something, they might not think I was suspicious.

Maybe the affair thing could still work. I'd personally apologize, stay over, people would see me a few times, then the fire, and he'd come stay with me. I needed him to cooperate. I wasn't about to roofie the guy, but I needed him to sleep with me of his own free will. My seduction game needed to be on point, and it would be. Alex was now a conquest, too—specifically for the purpose of killing him.

I jogged again that night after dinner, physically running into Alex.

"Oh!" I looked up after smacking my forehead in someone's chest. "Oh, Alex! I'm so sorry! Honestly."

"It's okay, Ms. Cage. Though, I'm beginning to think you may be stalking me," he joked.

I laughed with him. "No, just extra stress lately. Extra stress makes for longer jogs."

"Well, would you like to come in and rest a bit? I've been meaning to call you, anyway." He fumbled with his keys as he walked to the door.

"You know…Yes, yes I would. Thank you, Alex." I smiled.

He opened the door and motioned for me to enter. "Up the stairs on the right."

"Got it."

I felt his eyes on me, and I would have been lying if I said they didn't feel good. We reached the top, and I stepped aside so he could unlock the door. I followed him in as he held the door open for me. *A gentleman.*

He locked the door behind us, and I couldn't figure out what his game was. As he took his coat off and hung it in the closet, I asked him why he wanted to talk to me.

"Because I changed my mind, Ms. Cage."

"Call me Britney, please." I blushed.

I sat on the couch. It was comfortable. Alex crossed through the living room into the kitchen, pouring a glass of water then grabbing himself a beer.

"Oh, if you don't mind, I'll take a beer too, please. I drink enough water during the day, I think I'd enjoy the change," I lied.

"Sure," Alex replied, putting the glass of water in the fridge and taking out another beer.

He came and sat next to me, handing me a beer. "Brit-ney—" He sounded unsure of addressing me by my first name, "I'm sorry I turned you down earlier. I guess I was just shocked that a woman like you would want someone like me."

"What does that mean? Am I better than you or something? No. You need to get that bullshit out of your head right now. No one is above you. Remember that," I lied. I lifted my beer in a toast, and he tapped it with his.

"So, would we be dating or…?"

"I don't date, per se. I prefer friends with benefits. I'll be honest: I've wanted you since I first met you. I was glad when Osten took you for himself. That meant I could flirt with, and hit on, you. Then you turned me down, so I thought you were already seeing someone."

"Ha!" Alex let out a belly laugh. "You must have me mixed up with someone else. But really? All this time?"

"Yeah. And about the flowers, you crossed a line just showing up at my house like that. Not cool, man. I *am* sorry I flipped out, but that scared the shit out of me." I batted my eyes at him as I set my beer on a coaster on the coffee table.

Alex apologized did the same, then kissed me. We had a hot and heavy makeout session on the couch. Then he took me back to his room, taking our clothes off as we went.

Neither of us cared that I was sweaty and sticky from jogging. Alex was much more passionate about the sex than I was, and I fell asleep in his arms. I woke up around two a.m. checked to make sure Alex was still sleeping, and tiptoed into the kitchen. I pulled the toaster oven away from the corner he'd placed it in, appalled he'd taken up valuable counter space that way. Unplugging it, I checked the cord. There was already a small tear in the plastic coating, exposing wire. plucked at it with my fingernails, fraying it, and put it back in the corner plugged in.

Twenty

ALEX WOKE UP AND kissed my forehead. I opened my eyes and smiled. So far, my plan was working. I had the futon in the den ready to go, along with an explanation of why he had to sleep on the futon. I'd already expressed "friends with benefits," and that was my simple reason for his needing to sleep on the futon. Maybe I'd be nice enough to take him to work, too. That part wasn't terribly important.

"How did you sleep?" he asked.

"Weird. I was up a bit, but I guess that's because I'm not in my own bed." I smiled seductively. "I wish I could stay, but I need to get home and get ready for work."

"Can't you play hooky?"

"No, and neither can you. Osten wouldn't be too happy about his only insurance person calling out."

"He told you?"

"Of course he did. He wanted to thank me again for sending you his way. He thinks you're great. More reasons why you can't play hooky yet." I got out of bed and put my clothes back on.

Alex did, too, coming to walk me to the door. "You sure you don't want to stay for coffee?" He grinned.

"Another day," I promised.

We kissed before I left, and my pulse quickened on my way out after he'd closed his door. With any luck, breakfast today was gonna be a scorcher.

I jogged back home, thinking how this would play out. Alex would start his morning toast, causing a fire. How much damage done would be decided by how quickly he could get to, and use, the extinguisher. If it got too bad, there was a fire alarm in the hall he could pull to get everyone else out. I hoped it wouldn't come to that, I guess.

I got home, showered, and finished my routine. By the time I'd gotten to the office, Julie was already there looking worried.

"What's wrong?"

"That Alex guy…"

"What about him? Did he get creepy on you?"

"No. He just called to let you know he had a fire. At his apartment. There's damage. He said he tried to call your cell but got your voice mail."

"Oh no! I'll have to call him and make sure he's okay."

I walked into my office, hung my coat, and closed the door. I didn't want Julie finding out about the affair just yet. I'd be questioned anyway because I stayed at his place last night. The affair would come out on its own—after they eventually found his rotting corpse—and I'd be a suspect. But only for a short period. I'd leave them nothing to go on other than that. I'd have a rock-solid alibi from the most prestigious people in the city saying that I was at the party.

A week and a half to go. That's all I had left, and it was going to be slow. It's always when you're excited about or anticipating something that time seems to nearly freeze.

I unlocked my computer and looked up Alex's cell number. Then I picked up the receiver and dialed. It rang twice before he answered.

"Hey, Brit."

"Hey. I just got in. Are you okay?"

"Yeah, I'm fine. I had an extinguisher in the kitchen anyway. I put it out as I was on the phone with dispatch. But half the kitchen is toast, literally," he chuckled. "Kind of funny, huh? I guess it's good I didn't offer you breakfast, too."

"So, what did the fire department say?"

"Well, they're still investigating, but it looks like my toaster oven is what started it. That thing was old anyway, and I planned to replace it. The insurance adjuster will be out here tomorrow. I don't think Dr. Osten is going to be very happy with me." He sounded worried.

"Calm down. Have you called him already?"

"No, I'm kind of afraid. I was hoping you might be so kind to…" He raised his tone at the end, more asking than stating.

I smiled. "Of course, I will. Do you need a place to stay? I have a spare bedroom."

He was silent for a few minutes. "That would be great. Brit, why are you so good to me?"

Because I'm going to kill you. "Because you're a great guy." I clenched my teeth so hard it hurt.

"You'll really call Dr. Osten for me?"

"As soon as we hang up. So you need today and tomorrow off. Any other days?"

"No. I can move my clothes and necessities over tonight. Well, as soon as I'm allowed back inside."

"Is there anything else I can do?"

"Doesn't look that way. Thanks, Brit. I really appreciate it."

"No problem. I'll text you after I talk to Osten."

"Okay. Call you when they let me back in."

"Sounds good. If you need anything else between now and then, call me."

"Okay. Thanks again. Bye, Brit."

I hung up the phone. He'd thanked me twice in less than ten seconds. I got it: The dude's apartment caught fire, thanks to my assistance…Then again, I think I'd be grateful if someone I barely knew offered the kind of help I had. I couldn't be mad at that, but I was still annoyed. He was always so polite that it made my skin crawl. *No one* on this planet was that polite these days. Alex was the exception. I wished there were more people like him, but he still needed to go.

I called Osten's cell phone and informed him of Alex's situation. He told me that he'd pay Alex both days, and to have Alex call him.

"He's a great employee, but he's so afraid to talk to me. Am I that intimidating?"

"I don't think so, but people say the same about me."

I called Julie's desk on threeway. "Julie, you're on with Dr. Osten."

"Hi, Doctor! How are you?" Julie perked up.

"I'm fine, and you?"

"Great! What can I do for you?"

"Julie," I started, "are we intimidating? 'We' meaning both Dr. Osten and I."

"When I first met you, Brit, yes, you were. Same for you, Doc. But now that I know both of you, I'd call you if I needed you."

"So how long after meeting Dr. Osten did you feel comfortable talking to him?"

"Maybe a week? He's a second dad to you, Brit. Doc, you're almost like an uncle to me."

I almost cried at that statement. The closer I got to killing Alex, the stronger my emotions were generally. "Okay, thanks, Julie."

I ended the call and went back to Osten. "I get why Alex is terrified. He's only been working for you for, what, a month? It makes sense. And you are intimidating at first. I'm so grateful you took me in as one of your own, but I still get weird around you."

We both laughed. He told me I'd better be at the barbecue and apologized for having to cut the conversation short.

I called Alex back and relayed what Osten told me.

"He said I can call him?" Alex was in shock.

"You work for the man; yes, you can call him. He won't yell at you. He's actually cooler than you think," I reassured him.

"Okay. I will on my way to your house."

"Whoa! You're not planning to tell him where you're staying, are you?" I flinched.

"No! We need to keep this quiet—"

"You're right. NO ONE is to know. Julie will be the only person to know anything because you already called and she's my know-everything person. Just don't tell her personal stuff, okay?"

Alex laughed. "Got it. Call you later."

"Bye." I put the receiver down. I looked up to see Julie leaning against the doorframe, a smirk on her face.

Twenty-One

JULIE STARED AT ME. I wasn't sure if it was shock on her face or amusement. I wanted to put my head down like a puppy in trouble, instead choosing to defiantly look her in the eye. I think that amused her more because she started to chuckle under her breath, still smirking; she couldn't help herself.

I let my impatience show. "What?"

Julie shrugged, and covered her mouth. She thought this whole thing with Alex more than amusing. I remembered her comment about needing to get laid and started to laugh. She joined in.

"*Now* I see why you said you didn't need help getting some," Julie snorted.

"Oh, hush." I laughed and waved her away.

I'd told Alex that Julie was the only person allowed to know he was staying with me, but now she knew way earlier than I'd planned to tell her. All because I failed to cover my tracks and close my door. A small mistake with possibly big implications. That worried me about the state of my Alex plan. What else had I missed?

Maybe I was being paranoid. Julie was a smart girl, so I knew she'd figure it out sooner than later, anyway. I just hadn't expected this soon.

Alex called around eleven saying he was on his way to come get my house keys to drop his stuff off. I said I'd meet him there—I wasn't sure how much I trusted him alone today. Luckily, all my research books were hidden in the safe, which was locked, in my closet. I'd have to log out of my streaming accounts where my twisted searches showed as soon as you turned it on. No big deal. This would only last a few, painfully long, weeks more.

Alex showed up about twenty minutes after calling—despite my telling him I'd meet him at my place. The little prick. And then the little fucker walked into the office like he owned the place.

"Is she available?" he asked Julie. No hello. No good afternoon. No "How are you?" Like I said, like *he* owned the place. This little fuck who rode the bus at nearly thirty and who probably still wore Mommy's dresses when he beat off. Like *he* owned the place. The gall.

If Julie hadn't been there, I swear to God I would have gutted him right there in my waiting room. Then I'd have turned my knife on that little worm he called a dick.

Julie messaged me over the computer, snapping me out of it, to let me know he was here. I messaged back, telling her to have him wait. Then, I heard Julie say, "She's in the middle of something. Take a seat."

I couldn't help but giggle. I sounded a little evil, even to me, which made my smile that much bigger. But Alex would have to get used to that, fast.

I don't take too much pleasure in fucking with people because I hated when it was done to me, but Alex deserved it, if only for the way he walked in here. And for his disrespect.

Five minutes later, I walked into the main office. I hugged Alex and apologized for what he'd been through. He told me the fire inspector had deemed it an accident, and his insurance company would have it fixed up in about a week.

One week, eh? That's perfect. In a week and a half, he dies, so I'm fully in the clear. All I need now is a place to do it.

Instead of giving Alex my keys, I went with him. Julie squeaked, thinking I'd be back near quitting time, and I let her think it. We got into Alex's Honda and drove to his apartment. On the ride, we made small talk, including his schedule for today and tomorrow. I cringed, thinking he'd probably want a key because he'd be in and out, but I didn't have much else of a choice. It was either that or make the neighbors think I was a whack who made guests wait outside for her to come home.

Not that I even knew my neighbors. Okay, maybe a name or two. There was this one nosy old bitch, but I honestly didn't need to worry about that. In a week, he'd be under my blade. Until then, that nosy old bitch, along with the rest of them, could think whatever they wanted. I literally did not care. They were all beneath me.

Alex pulled into my driveway, and I unlocked the front door as he grabbed two duffels and a backpack. Did he really need two full duffel bags? I didn't ask out loud because I simply didn't care to know, regardless how much it gnawed at my curiosity.

I gave Alex the tour, including the den, where he'd be sleeping. He liked it. Not like he had much choice. I smiled to myself.

I gave him the spare key, and he drove me back to the office. He tried kissing me bye, but I got out before he even came to a full stop. I'm somewhat good like that. The rest of the time, I was rather clumsy. To put it nicely, I was no James Bond.

Julie just watched me, expression flat, as I walked back in.

"It's not funny," I stated flatly.

She broke out into a wide grin. "But it is! Come on, look out the door. That dude wanted a kiss, and you bailed faster than a hooker jumps on money."

"Wow, Jules. I definitely wasn't expecting that from you." I laughed.

"I learned it from watching you." We both laughed at that. Old-school commercials were hilariously earnest.

I let her know Alex had the other spare key to my house—she had one in case I went away. Not that I'd be taking any vacations with Alex around. I'd have to do my nighttime searching somehow and without waking him up. The only thing I could come up with at the moment was to tell him I was out with the girls. He didn't know them and wouldn't feel like he could call them.

Sure, he could call my cell and track it, which I wouldn't put past him, but I didn't think he was that clever. At least, that's what I was banking on. I needed a warehouse or something else abandoned with no neighbors to complain about the noise or seeing me driving in or out.

I hadn't thought this through It wasn't like my others. Those had been meticulously planned. I was slipping and didn't know why.

I wasn't new to the area; I wasn't new to any of this. I didn't keep notes because those would be one of the things that would prove my guilt. But maybe I needed to start. Handwritten notes burned as each bit was carried out. What choice did I have at this point?

My memory wasn't failing; I was. I wouldn't tolerate failure. This was too huge a fuckup to accept. I'd have to fix this. Maybe I'd start tonight. Alex would still be getting settled in, and I'm sure, be exhausted. He'd mentioned going to work today, even if only for an hour, and I'd already told him Osten was paying him to take as much time as he needed.

Alex didn't care; he couldn't stand the thought of falling behind in his work.

I called Alex before leaving the office to head home.

"Hey," he answered.

"Hey. I'm leaving the office. Want me to pick up dinner?"

"Nah. Thanks, though. I'm gonna pick up some food on my way into the office."

"Uh, you know the girls locked up, right?" I was confused.

"I called Dr. Osten, and he agreed to let me come in while the cleaning people was there, but I have to leave when they do. I don't want to fall too far behind. Paperwork won't wait but phone calls can."

"If you say so. All right. Well then, I guess I'll see you when you get back. If it's after ten, please don't make a lot of noise You'll wish you'd never met me if you wake me up." I chuckled.

Alex did too, not realizing that I basically turned into a dragon if someone woke me up.

We ended our call, and I grabbed my things. Julie waited for me at the front door, making kissy faces.

"Shut it." I laughed. "You're the one getting hot and heavy."

Julie blushed. "I am, so what?"

"I'm happy for you. Honestly happy for you. You deserve a good guy."

We hugged and left the office, me locking the door. I unlocked my Jeep and jumped up into the driver's seat. No hanging with the crawlers tonight. That would have to wait. Tonight, I'd find my kill chamber.

Twenty-Two

OUTSIDE DOWNTOWN, YBOR WAS no good place at night. It was, however, perfect for what I needed. Something far enough away from the housing and close enough to the train tracks that no one would hear anything. I had some supplies ready to go: rubber gloves, contractor bags, a razor to cut them with, peroxide. I needed running water, preferably hot, since I didn't want to bring my favorite stainless travel tumbler into this. I could barely contain myself yet somehow managed. If I couldn't find a place with hot water, I'd have to use a portable grill and a pot or something to heat it up. The surefire way to make blood stains permanently disappear was a peroxide-and-water mix. I wasn't sure duct tape was how I wanted to proceed, with few exceptions, so I'd need chains, too. And, obviously, something to chain Alex to. I was still debating the torture thing.

I parked at a building with no signage, one I knew to be a crematorium, and walked around, dodging streetlights. I'd only had sneakers in my Jeep, so I'd changed shoes at a red light. I kept cursing myself for not having dark clothes in the back—I *always* had a change of clothes for jogging. I was disappointed in myself for this, another small mistake, but it made me more determined.

Alex had a week left to live, and some part of me hoped he'd live it up. I knew he wouldn't, though. He didn't socialize and cared only about work and not letting Osten down. At least he'd be out of my hair and stop annoying me. Even Julie thought he was creepy, so I had that going for me, too.

Building after building, I found more homeless than I'd imagined I would. Seeing them made me wish I'd brought food and drinks. Giving them anything, however, might make them say something if the cops ever came around. My Jeep didn't hide easily. I'd planned to bring Alex down here in his own car, having mine already inside whichever building I chose. Or I could leave it out by that tank place and drop Alex's car somewhere, but that would make the cops go looking. No, there was a junkyard around here. I'd drop it off and pay someone to keep their mouth shut, with the promise of a long and painful death if they didn't.

After that happy thought left my mind, I quite literally stumbled upon a building that, from the outside, looked perfect. I poked my way through a hole in the metal wall next to the locked garage door.

The inside was bare except for a few office chairs or wheels, a bunch of car repair equipment, and more office furniture, like desks. I could work with a wheeled chair, so long as I had a chain.

I walked around, using the flashlight on my phone, and found some dead rats, another garage door on the side, and an old chain. There was also a parts-washing station that was dismantled somehow. I could use this for washing the chain before dumping the car. I'd have to wrap the body and make sure he didn't leak blood everywhere. Transporting still-bleeding bodies was the worst.

Peroxide wreaked havoc on vehicle interiors and, unless disposed of properly, could be tested for the presence of other chemicals. I started to wonder if Alex was worth all this trouble and if I shouldn't just knock off one of these homeless instead.

I had one tiny problem gnawing at that thought: I was more stubborn than a bull. Once my mind was made up, I didn't budge. Anyway, I guess I could leave the pencil in his ear for minimal leakage. Maybe even wrap some gauze around his head, topped off with a contractor bag…

My plan was finally falling into place, I hoped. I now had a kill garage, not just a chamber. It was possible I could use this place again, but not immediately. I walked back out of the same hole I'd come in through, walking to the side of the building with the other garage door. This one was also locked. Even better that it was covered by complete darkness. This was my official way in. I rubbed my hands together like a greedy old man you'd see in a pre-1990 movie. My night had just been made.

I got home and saw Alex's car parked against the curb in front of my house. *So fucking polite! Also a good way for me to walk in the house happy and not mad at him. I still refused to give him kudos on the basis of politeness alone. After all, it was his perfect little manners that had ensured his death.*

I shifted into park and got out, but not before changing back into the heels I had on in the office. I saw no need to give Alex reason to question me, except maybe about sex, which was easy enough to explain away. There would be none of that between now and Osten's barbecue. No condom residue on the broken body that would be found meant no leads. The cops would eventually come this way looking for him anyway, and I'd have no answers about his disappearance. No one would.

I opened the door and smelled garlic.

"Alex?" I closed the door and took my shoes off.

"Hey! In the kitchen. The pizza's almost ready."

I set my bag down and padded into the kitchen. Alex was bending over the open oven, pulling out a homemade white pie. I had to hand it to him this time. I didn't expect dinner when I got home, yet here it was. And it smelled amazing.

"What's the pizza for?"

"It's my way of thanking you for letting me stay here while my place gets fixed up." He set the tray on top of the stove to let it cool before cutting it. I went to the refrigerator and took out a bottle of Moscato. There was always a reason for a glass of wine. Sure, it would come up in the toxicology screen, but who didn't have at least a little alcohol in their system?

I set the bottle on the table, then got plates and glasses. Maybe we should celebrate a little tonight. I could celebrate my Job-like patience and Alex could celebrate…that he got to live another day.

He sliced the pizza and set the tray on the table on top of an oven mitt. I didn't have much in the way of plates to display entrees.

Alex pulled a chair out for me. I accepted graciously. The smell of the pizza was incredible.

"I didn't know you cooked," I remarked as Alex sat down.

"You never asked." He winked.

Ugh. I'm going to throw up. So polite and nice. Sure, the nice guy gets walked all over, but not him. He doesn't let anyone in far enough to walk on him. And soon, he'll never even be able to try.

Alex put a slice on my plate, then served himself. I poured the wine. Alex insisted on toasting me. I let him have it but didn't pay any attention to the words he was saying. I was lost in visions of what would take place in the warehouse. Maybe I'd do a property search just to see if anyone still owned it. If there was an owner and somehow it came to light that a murder took place there, the owner could potentially be questioned, though the place looked like it'd been left years ago.

I bit into my slice. Holy mouthgasm! Garlicky, but not too much, olive oil, just the right amount of alfredo sauce, topped with shredded parmesan. This was some damn good pizza. I'd have to get the recipe from Alex tonight. He smiled, sipped his wine, and went back to enjoying his slice.

When I was able to talk again, I asked him for the recipe, and he happily wrote it down. At least he realized he wouldn't be staying here forever and respected that. I placed it on the fridge with a magnet and smiled. Great food, good wine, and my prey all at the same table. Tonight couldn't get any better. And then it did.

Twenty-Three

JULIE CALLED, AND FOR once, I let it go to voice mail. Surprisingly, Alex and I were having fun drinking the rest of the wine I'd opened for dinner and doing the dishes. We laughed so hard it hurt, almost dropping the plates a few times. We laughed about that, too. Tonight, we'd enjoyed each other in the same ways we had when I'd spent the night at his apartment. We lay on the futon, my head on his shoulder, talking about his weird neighbor. As luck would have it, the lady who gave my information to the cops was the same lady who called them for a prowler in the first place. I made a mental note to call Officer What's-His-Name and put him in touch with Alex about her. Alex mentioned the woman was old, and alone. Sounded like my nosy old neighbor. Also, pretty paranoid—tin-foil-hat paranoid. Good thing I wasn't killing him at his apartment.

I rolled and stood up, intending to shower and go to sleep in my own bed. Alex didn't argue or ask what was going on with us, which I was grateful for. I hoped he wouldn't get attached.

Minion followed me, trying to trip me up the stairs out of sheer excitement. I picked her up when we reached the top, petting her and scratching her chin. I started the shower and let it warm up as I grabbed my towels. I was confident Alex wouldn't try to slip in with me, but I closed and locked my bedroom door anyway. I couldn't trust someone I considered prey, whether they were sleeping under my roof or not. And my .380 was in my nightstand. I may have snored, but I was not a terribly heavy sleeper. If Alex tried to come in, I'd hear it and shoot him. Not that I could claim self-defense because the cops would wonder why I let someone I didn't trust sleep just below me in the first place. I imagined the conversation:

"So, you let a guy you didn't trust sleep in your house?"

"Yes. His apartment had a small fire, so while it was being fixed, I let him stay here. He was polite enough, and I know his boss. Besides, I planned to kill him anyway, so I guess it's cool, right?"

Jesus, that sounded dumb even in my head!

I stood under the hot water longer than usual, contemplating killing Alex here. But that didn't make sense, either. I could find deadly flowers that would break down in his system long before they even took blood for toxicology, but that would require me to leave the house.

A lot could go bad really quickly, like my nosy old neighbor watching. She and I never quite saw eye-to-eye, and she was retired with nothing else to do but bitch about stupid little things.

I washed my hair and continued thinking. Not that I knew why since I had figured it all out tonight. All that was truly left was to make sure I was seen by everyone at the party and to slip out unnoticed. I knew I couldn't be gone long, but it didn't take long to get from South Tampa to Ybor on a Saturday night.

I washed my face and body and turned the shower off, grabbing my towel at the same time. Minion sat on the counter, judging me for not petting her. She decided to come to me and get her pets in, me ending up with a handful of cat fur.

I laughed and shook my head, continuing to dry off. Minion had other plans. She wanted me covered in as much fur as possible, so she rubbed against my legs every chance she got. I broke away, hung up my towel, and changed into my pajamas. Minion met me on my pillow. I gently moved her so we could share, though she really did prefer my hair. Apparently, not tonight. She curled up where my neck meets my jaw, moved some of my hair around, and passed out. I giggled, petted her, and managed a selfie without waking her up or dropping my phone. I turned the streaming app to one of my background-noise shows and drifted off.

I woke to the smell of coffee and bacon. I didn't remember buying bacon on my last shopping trip, so I shook it off.

Then I smelled French toast. This was getting a little crazy, but I'd have been lying if I didn't admit I felt that I deserved to be treated this way, even if only for another morning or two. Even by a worm I would soon kill.

The clock read 6:41 a.m. I already felt like I was going to be late, but I also knew how to nicely brush anyone off when necessary. I got downstairs and turned the corner to see the kitchen and table. My mouth about fell open at the spread: coffee, bacon, juice, bagels, eggs. This was too much from someone who would never be my boyfriend, let alone see Sunday morning. Again, came that voice from the back of my head telling me I worked too hard to be where I was, and that I deserved this. I smiled and walked to the table, sitting in my chair.

There was a fresh cup of coffee and a glass of juice in front of me. I went for the coffee first; the juice would be for when I ate.

Alex was still making eggs, so I waited for him to put food on my plate. I rarely ate breakfast, but all of it smelled so good that my stomach started grumbling. I wasn't sure if Alex had noticed me enter, so I piped up.

"You made all of this for me?" I asked, my voice going up an octave or two.

"*Us*, I made it for us. I forgot to ask how you liked your eggs last night, so I just went with scrambled. I hope that's okay." He turned from the stove and grinned at me.

I returned the smile and nodded. "It is. Thank you for doing this."

He turned around looking like a stern father, waving the spatula at me, fake voice and all. "Just like I told you last night, this is my way of thanking you for letting me stay here. You barely know me, but here you are, my housing savior, and former employer."

I toasted him with my coffee, and we both laughed. My internal voice laughed maniacally. *You fool. You might want to say your goodbyes now.* I shook my head and grabbed a bagel and the cream cheese. As I spread it on, my mouth started before I had time to think.

"Hey, Alex? Did you go out and get this stuff?"

"I did. And, no, you're not giving me money back for it." He brought the last of the eggs over and sat down.

That explained a lot. He was genuinely so polite, so guarded, that he believed I was doing him a favor. He'd spend the rest of his life getting walked on like a doormat if I didn't do this for him.

I now realized it wasn't just for me. It was to be a mercy killing. There was no need for the man to suffer if he didn't

have to. And being as polite as he was, being walked on *was* suffering.

Whether he realized it or not, he was suffering. He had no one in his life except coworkers and barely there family. He didn't even have me.

Twenty-Four

A WEEK. I WAS mentally counting down the days and hours until I could let my bloodlust out to play. I got goose bumps when I thought about it. I'd leave the party after making sure everyone just saw me and, according to whoever "just saw" me, I'd gone to mingle with so-and-so. It would trickle down the line until there wasn't any time I wasn't accounted for. Osten would even make something up, if he had to. He'd say he put me in one of the guest rooms to sleep and checked on me every so often because I was drunk. I don't think he'd protect me if he knew what I was truly up to or who I actually was. I've said before, I don't want anyone else involved or knowing. It puts me at a higher risk for getting caught, and it puts them in danger as well. The last thing I wanted was to intentionally put someone I cared about in danger because they simply knew what I was. The one person who did is long dead. I regret it had to happen, but it was for her own good.

Anyway, I was letting Minion choose my outfit for the day, and she nosed a pair of black slacks and a floral top. I could work with that. The cat had good taste. I guess she got it from watching me. I know, it sounds crazy that a cat picks out my clothes, but today she really did a good job. I can't say that about every other time. Most times, she throws her nose in the air like the spoiled princess she was. I pulled the items off their hangers and put them on. Basic black pumps would work with this combo. I smiled and turned for the bathroom to finish getting ready.

Alex called up the stairs, but it was muffled because my door was closed and locked. Minion hated it, and so did I, but it was temporary. I ignored him, and my phone went off. It was a text from Alex. He didn't want to leave for the day without saying bye. I texted back that I was almost done and would be down in a few minutes.

The bus from here only took a few more minutes than from his place. The stops were spread out in a weird way, but from south Tampa to Northdale, the ride was an hour and change. He wasn't going that far and, honestly, I could've taken him, but he insisted he take the bus. Fine by me. That just meant we wouldn't be seen together, and I was more than okay with that. I finished up and went downstairs. Minion followed, even rubbing up against Alex once or twice. He bent down to pet her, and she ran for her food bowl. Having Alex here messed up my morning routine, but I'd have to tell my quirky mind to shut up and deal with it. I followed Minion so I could feed her, and Alex followed me.

"What's up? I gave you a key, right?"

"Yeah, thanks. And thanks again for letting me stay here."

"If you don't stop thanking me—" I tried to joke, but Alex kissed me midsentence. I pushed him off.

"Whoa, man! Don't do that. We're not dating. We're friends with occasional benefits. Don't go catching feelings, either. You'll trip and hurt yourself. I'm happy not being in a committed relationship. I have things I want to do before I settle down, if that ever happens."

Alex put his hands up. "I get it. I'm sorry. I'll see you later." He turned and took off out the door. I hoped that nosy old bat didn't see him, or I'd be fucked.

I continued into the kitchen to feed Minion before I left. Alex had done all the dishes—dried and put them away. He was a great houseguest. It was a real shame what I had to do to him.

I almost started to feel bad about it, then I reminded myself this was a mercy killing and he'd be so much better off. Not that his happiness or suffering was anything for me to decide, but how much did it hurt if I helped that decision along?

Minion yelled at me for her pets before I left.

"Oh, little girl. What am I gonna do with you?" I kissed her nose and scratched her chin before grabbing my purse and jacket.

When I arrived, Julie's car wasn't in the lot, and the front door was still locked. *Weird. She hasn't texted or called, either.* I unlocked the door and locked it behind me. I wasn't quite prepared to open, so I left the lights off too. As I hung my purse, I realized I never checked the voice mail Julie left last night. I set the phone on my desk and played the message on speaker. Julie said she'd be late, something about a doctor appointment, and she'd be in by ten.

"Huh," I said out loud and deleted the message. Julie sounded excited and scared, all at once. She was probably pregnant and considering abortion or something. I'd be there for her no matter what it was, regardless. She was my protégé and friend. If we weren't so close in age, I'd have felt like she was my daughter. I was motherly to her at times. I had no doubt that when she came in, she'd let me know what was going on.

I started my computer, then went to unlock the doors and turn the lights on. The office was boring without Julie there, so I moped my way around opening. Back at my desk, I checked the voice mail. Nothing interesting, just solicitations for updating the address for the internet phone book and another robocall IRS scam. I deleted them and hung up the phone.

I'd been at my computer working and scanning in new paperwork for what felt like an eternity when Julie came bouncing in the front door. The chimes went off, and she giggled, said sorry, and came straight into my office. She sat down in front of me and smiled this eerily large smile and waited for my eyes to meet hers.

When I looked up at her, I smiled. She looked like a little kid losing their first tooth. She laughed with me, then teared up.

"Oh no. What's wrong?" I grabbed the box of tissues from my drawer and set it down in front of her.

"Oh God, nothing's wrong. It's all perfect." She was gushing and glowing.

I cocked my head to the side, like a confused dog would. Julie laughed and leaped out of her chair. She came around the desk and sat on my lap. This was a first.

"Are you a Pod Person? What have you done with my Julie? Give her back!" I picked up a pencil, ready to stab the obvious impostor.

Julie laughed again and showed me her left hand. My mouth dropped open in awe. For a bartending college student, Cody sure knew how to pick a diamond. I wrapped my arms around her so tightly, I thought I might break her.

"Congratulations! Have you set a date?"

"No." She shook her head. "We want to live together first as an engaged couple. You know, to make sure we don't kill each other." She giggled.

"But why engaged? You could live together without—"

"The promise," she finished for me.

My face went blank. I understood the promise and wanting to have it. I'd never had it; I'd chased it away and actively avoided it. But I was so happy for her. Julie deserved all the happiness the universe would give her.

I now fully understood why she and Cody wanted to be engaged a while before getting married. It wasn't about the money he spent on the ring; it was about them making decisions together and promising each other now, before the vows. I hugged her again, both of us shedding tears of joy. I pushed her back and smiled.

"Julie, the world is yours, and happiness belongs to you. Let me throw a party when you're ready, huh?"

Her face turned even redder, and she cried. "I couldn't…No…Brit—"

"So, that's a yes. Got it." I smirked at her. She knew I wasn't taking no for an answer. "If I'd ever wanted children, I'd have hoped they would be just like you."

She stood from my lap, mumbling about she had to get to work, laughed, and walked out of my office. I watched her go, then closed the door.

I was so happy for her, but I had to call Officer What's-His-Name. I looked around and found the message in my pen drawer. *Officer Sweet.* I picked up the phone and dialed.

Twenty-Five

SWEET'S VOICE MAIL PICKED up, so I left him a message about the old lady. I also left Alex's name and number, adding, "You asked me to call if I had any information for you. Have a good day." I hoped this would put more of whatever investigation he had going onto the crackpot old lady. She was a fucking nuisance, a thorn in my side. I didn't need her fucking this up for me. Alex would die. By my hands. It irked me that no one else was bothered by how incessantly polite that skinny shit was.

I turned on the radio, let the station play, and got to work. I had payroll to get done. It usually took me about three hours but today I felt sluggish; must've been eating breakfast that made me want to take a nap. *Dammit, Alex.* I should probably tell him the breakfast thing needs to stop.

Shaking the drowsiness from my head, I opened the time-keeping system and got to work. I had to update everyone, including those who hadn't been available. They all checked in through an app or website with their availability. I had it synced so that when someone changed their availability, the payroll system would update itself, but it'd been glitchy lately and I kept putting off calling my computer guy. I wrote myself a note, then stuck it on my monitor to remind me to call him after I was finished.

The morning continued at a snail's pace. I even sent Julie for our favorite mochas and lattes. I asked for mine to be a quad shot. Julie didn't ask why, simply smiled at my exhausted face and left. She had to suspect something; how could she not? I couldn't remember the last time I came in like this and continued to flop throughout the day. Julie always picked up on things, even slight changes. If I sneezed wrong, she was coming at me with cold medicine and tissues.

She returned in record time and sat with me. We sipped our drinks in silence until I couldn't take her schoolgirl looks anymore.

"What? Why are you looking at me like that?"

Julie giggled and blushed. She didn't like to kiss and tell, and she sure didn't like getting into my business unless I freely told her.

"You look like crap, like you've been run over by a steamroller," she said, choosing her words not-so-carefully.

"I'm aware." I took a sip of my peppermint mocha. "And you can tell me I look like shit. I prefer the bluntness."

Julie blushed again. She was modest in that she was easily embarrassed, though she really was a pure innocent at heart. But damn, was she good with clients.

I'd forgotten how much I enjoyed watching Julie interact with those clients, current and prospective. She'd be amazing in my position. This was my way of sorting through people. Passing Through Temp Agency was just what the name indicated. Gruesome, I knew; however, I didn't care.

Most people saw it as a literal stop on their career path. And they weren't wrong. It's just that some didn't make it out for one reason or another. Maybe I was that reason; maybe I wasn't.

Instead of asking, Julie watched me carefully, trying to figure out why I was so tired. I read her face and answered her.

"Alex made breakfast this morning—bacon, eggs, bagels, the works. This steamrolled face is why I don't do breakfast. That, and it makes me hungry for the rest of the day."

"He made breakfast?" Julie's eyebrow arched.

"And dinner," I piped up.

Julie's face went into full shock.

"He says it's his way of thanking me for letting him stay. I say it's less on takeout, *and* I don't have to cook. I'm cool with it."

"You don't think it's creepy?"

"Nah. The guy's harmless. And a little old-fashioned, but so what? Besides, you forget I have my .380 in the nightstand.

Julie laughed. "Touché." She stood and went back to her desk for the remaining hour until lunch. Julie went out and so did I, though in opposite directions. She to food, me to Ybor. I needed to see the garage in the daylight; even a simple drive-by would do.

I made it there in record time for lunch-hour traffic. This proved how quickly I could get there on a Saturday night. And I wouldn't have to take toll roads, which weren't even an option in the first place because there were cameras at every on- and off-ramp. I had a SunPass, but I sure as shit also had a brain in my head. Even so, as an extra precaution, I wouldn't be in my car; I'd be driving Alex's. I could loan him the pass, but again, stupidity. I was already expecting to be questioned. No need to make it worse.

As I drove along, Tampa's infamous homeless shuffled about, panhandling or sharing food. The garage still looked like a great option for more than just Alex. I almost wanted to buy it, but then I'd seriously be in shit, big time, just because my name was on the deed. It wouldn't matter if I wasn't running a business out of it or leasing it out. My name meant my responsibility. That was too big a risk to take. Regardless, it wouldn't stop me from using it as needed, but not immediately. Kills there too close together would tip off authorities to a serial killer. Kills all in the same garage would saturate the entire area in cop and FBI patrols.

I drove my way back to the office, again in record time. Lunchtime traffic was almost as bad as rush hour, with what seemed like the entire tri-county area taking lunch at the exact same time. Julie beat me back, so the door was unlocked when I tried it. She gave me the messages from the hour, and I went back to my office to sort through them.

One was from Officer Sweet. Julie noted on the paper that she'd left the recording on the voice mail and that I should listen to it. I picked up the receiver and pressed the Voice Mail button. There was one message left. I pushed two to play it.

"Hi, Ms. Cage. It's Officer Sweet. Thanks for the information you left me. I'm familiar with the woman, and I've left Alex a message. Maybe we can do something about her thinking everyone is the devil, who knows. Thanks again and have a great day. I don't expect to need to speak with you again regarding this matter. Consider it handled, but please stay vigilant."

The recording ended, and I saved the message in case I needed it in the future. I thanked Julie for saving it and let her know I'd saved it as well. With him out of my hair now, I felt more confident about this weekend.

What I needed to figure out was an outfit. It was a casual affair, and the weather forecast didn't look that great. No one ever saw me in sneakers unless they caught me on a jog, plus there was no way in hell I'd wear sneakers to a professional event unless it was one of those mud races or something. I had a pair of Doc Martens that looked good with just about anything. They gave a grunge feeling but weren't totally nineties. I figured to pair them with jeans and a nice top. That settled that.

My cell went off. It was Alex thanking me for calling Officer Sweet and giving him Alex's number. I responded with "np" and went back to my computer. I didn't give a second thought about Alex texting after lunch, but hindsight was twenty-twenty.

Twenty-Six

ALEX TEXTING AFTER LUNCH meant he actually took a break. He barely took lunch, let alone a break. He dealt with insurance companies all day, which meant he was at their mercy. I expect he'd formed relationships with some people, at least a few by now, but that didn't explain the break. He was a creature of habit, and once a habit was formed, Alex didn't break from it. *Shit.* I couldn't figure out if this new development was a good or bad thing. Maybe he just had to pee and checked his phone in the process. He probably hoped for something from me or maybe the contractor. I know I'd have been eager to move back home, but he, more than likely, wasn't. He enjoyed staying with me and had secret hopes of us becoming a couple. I'd rained on that parade twice now, but I knew he wanted me.

I stopped wondering and made busywork to pass the time. Turns out, after payroll was finished today, I didn't have much else to do. So, I mentally plotted leaving the party Saturday, having Alex meet me at the garage in Ybor under the guise of steamy, dirty sex, and then the kill.

As I plotted, my imagination saw each move, each pivot—the kill—and even felt the high.

I imagined the drive to Melbourne and back; it would be slow and dull. Especially with my head and adrenaline

buzzing, fresh with the jitters of post-kill excitement. I wanted to take only back roads; however, I-4 seemed the most logical and quickest. I smiled at the image of dumping his body in the mud to be rolled over by a tank. I giggled a bit, too. *How are you going to contain yourself for another couple of days?* I laughed again.

My daydreams relaxed me the rest of the day, so I wasn't prepared for the shit storm that awaited. I got home just before Alex, and holy hell, was he pissed when he hit the door.

Apparently, he'd taken that break with the hopes of talking to me. About what he didn't say, but out of nowhere—again, with no encouragement from me—he had turned jealous, like psycho-stalker jealous. Like the kind of guy who'd try to kill me if I left him or kicked him out.

I wasn't scared, but it shocked me. I quickly realized that there was a lot more to Alex than I'd thought. A lot below the surface, brewing just under the brim. Seemed like he was about to boil over.

"I was hoping we could have a minute today," he spat, his tone edged with a coldness I hadn't heard before. "I took time out of my day because I wanted to 'thank you' and see if maybe I could change your mind about us."

Holy shit, he might be as crazy as I am.

"I was—"

"Don't you fucking interrupt me when I'm speaking to you!" He turned toward me fully, fist clenched, and started coming my way.

But this little worm had forgotten that I was the Alpha Female of the species. I'd wait to kill him, sure, but I was going to make him wish I would have.

"How dare you!" The venom in my voice scared Minion clear up to my bedroom. I walked forward to meet him before he stopped and glared at me. "I give you a place to stay...I'm *fucking you*! You KNEW my boundaries, and you wanna pull this bullshit? The fuck you will! There is no *us*! There's never going to be any *us*! If your place was finished, I'd throw you back in the hole I pulled you from the bottom of, you arrogant little—" I think both my volume and my obvious anger are what stopped him in his tracks.

My best-laid plans aside, if I had let myself continue, even finish that sentence, I'd have killed him there and then. That wasn't happening.

Thankfully, he backed down immediately like the cuck he was. He hung his head like a misbehaved dog who got caught and walked to the den, closing the door behind him. He knew he was in the wrong, and I hoped he genuinely felt bad.

I did, but only for scaring the shit out of my cat. I decided to take her food upstairs to her, thinking she may not come back down unless I did. I put food in her bowl, squeezed a little Churu on top, and took it upstairs.

Minion was sitting on the bed, almost expecting me to serve her. She wasn't scared at all, the little shit. She had known I'd feel guilty and would come, bowl in hand, with my peace offering. I shook my head laughing and set the bowl down in front of her.

While she ate, I changed clothes for a jog. I was too angry to eat or read, and I needed to take that negative energy out. One more sleep, not including tonight, and I could let my inner demon out to play. That was my sole comforting thought at the moment.

I jogged my usual route up Bayshore and back, feeling better. I wasn't about to have makeup sex with Alex—it wasn't that great in the first place—but I did want a shower. You didn't jog in Florida and not sweat unless it was cold, which was two weeks a year. Luckily, and surprisingly, the humidity hadn't kicked in yet. It was a normal thing for March to start acting up weather-wise, yet we had lucked out this year. I was grateful for it because it meant less money I had to spend on a gym membership just to use the treadmill. I don't know why I never bought one. Probably because they're clunky and take up more space than I'm willing to give up. I'd probably already bought four or five with my gym-membership fees.

I showered and went to bed happy, ignoring Alex, who no doubt would be sulking all night in the den. Minion curled up with me, as usual. And we fell asleep, both of us snoring.

My alarm went off, signaling Friday morning. One more day of this, and Alex was mine in ways he'd never dreamed. I went about my morning routine, Alex texting to see if I was willing to talk to him. He apologized in that text, too.

You're driving me crazy! I want to pull my hair out! I straightened and finished up. When I got downstairs, there was coffee ready and no breakfast. *Thank fucking God.*

Alex was sitting at the table, lost in staring at his full mug. I poured some for myself and sipped, then walked over to the table.

"Apology accepted. But this you-staying-here thing is old. Have you heard from the contractors?"

Alex nodded. "I have. I already called Dr. Osten and asked for the day off to move back home and make sure everything's fixed properly."

"Perfect. Not that I need to explain myself, but I hope you see why I don't want a relationship with anyone. I don't tolerate anyone making rules for me. I make the rules."

Alex nodded again. No words came out of his mouth. I was relieved…until I wasn't.

"I'm sorry. My things are packed and already in my car. I really do appreciate you giving me a place to crash and everything else you've done for me." He chugged his lukewarm coffee and continued, "I'll be going now." He never picked his head up or made eye contact. He set his mug in the sink and left.

I didn't take the bait and let him walk right out the front door.

"Whew!" I let out once he closed the door behind himself. Minion rubbed against my leg and mewed. It seemed to always be feeding time. For me, that would be tomorrow night. And now I had the perfect lure for Alex to meet me. I was feeling devious and scrappy, but all that had to wait. A smile spread across my face as I fed Minion and walked out the door myself.

On my way to the office, I rocked out to songs like "My Demons" by Starset and "Scream, Aim, Fire" by Bullet for My Valentine. The windows were down, and my hair blew all around, and there I was, acting like I was seventeen again. Tomorrow I'd feel alive.

Not that I felt dead. On the contrary, I always felt a sense of being and belonging and comfort in my humanity. I was a good person, no matter how many I'd killed—and would continue to kill.

I loved life—well, my own life, anyway—and I worked hard to keep it the way it was. I was proud of what I'd accomplished, and so were my parents. It would break their hearts to know their little girl was a serial killer. I planned for them to be in their graves by the time I got caught, but I also held no illusions: accidents happen, and people slip up.

I parked at the office, turning the radio down, and putting the windows up. I walked with a bounce in my step that I couldn't shake.

Julie's face lit up when I walked in. "Did you get some hubba bubba last night?" She blushed and giggled.

"Nope. Alex and I argued because he was acting like a jealous boyfriend. But his apartment is finished, so he went home. That's why I'm so happy. Who knew having a houseguest for a week would really go so far south so fast?"

I bounced my way into my office, happily getting to work.

Twenty-Seven

THE WORKDAY ENDED, BUT before we left for the weekend, I asked Julie if I could take her out to celebrate. The celebration was actually for me, but she excitedly agreed. We took our own vehicles to remind us not to get drunk. We went to Applebee's for half-price happy hour. It was nice getting two drinks for the price of one, but even better were the half-price appetizers. We each ordered the pretzel sticks with beer cheese and boneless wings in two flavors, and I ordered the spinach and artichoke dip. I was a sucker for it anywhere I went. The bartender asked for our order, and I got a dirty martini—or two, as it were—and Julie ordered a cosmo. Two-for-one deals usually meant watered down unless it was beer we ordered. When the bartender came back, she took our food order and laughed.

"You two will not eat all of that! Or will you?"

I laughed. "I'm a bottomless pit, and so is she. Worst case is a doggy bag, right?" I winked, and we all laughed.

Julie told me how moving was going. They were on the hunt for a bigger place, and they were looking to rent.

"Why didn't you tell me? You know I've got the best contacts," I poked.

"I didn't really want to ask any special favors." Julie looked down into her drink sheepishly.

"On please. Call whomever you want. You don't need me as a reference since they all know you, but if you do need a reference, I'm always happy to provide one."

"Won't most of them be at Dr. Osten's tomorrow," Julie asked as she chewed her straw.

"You're right; they will." I smiled and hugged her. I really was genuinely happy for her. And proud of her. She already knew we'd network at the party, but that was her way of asking permission, to make sure it was the smart move. She returned the hug and held on a little too tightly.

I gently pushed her to arm's length. "What's wrong?"

"Nothing," she sniffled, "but I have one last thing to ask."

I started to get worried. Was she about to ask me to be her baby's godmother or something? Oh shit, if she was pregnant…I forced myself to stop being selfish. If she wanted to have a baby now, I'd give them the world.

"Will you be my maid of honor?" Julie asked, cheeks puffy and pink.

"You're damn right I will! Does that mean you've set a date?"

She shook her head as she sipped her drink.

The food arrived as Julie calmed down. We clinked glasses and sipped and ate and enjoyed ourselves. We talked about a seriously low-key bachelorette party. One where we sat around in our pajamas watching scary movies, like a sleepover party. We were big kids and enjoyed every second of it. Tonight would be a good time, tomorrow too. Tomorrow night would be even better.

My brain kept wandering to images of being in the garage and killing Alex. They were savory images, but so was the food.

Julie and I chatted about things she wanted for the wedding; I offered to help her plan. My gift would be helping her pay for either the wedding or the honeymoon. Of course, she wouldn't know until she argued with me about it. I was sneaky that way, and I truly loved Julie. She was like family to me, and I'm good to family as much as I can be.

We finished our food and drinks and parted ways for the night, agreeing to meet at Osten's tomorrow. She was a mixture of excited and tired, while I was simply excited. I went home, changed into sweats and a ball cap, and went to the garage.

In a turn of serendipity, I found chains lying around. They were dirty and gross. First, I tried the parts washer, but it was empty—parts cleaner dries like rubbing alcohol. So, I threw the chains in a contractor bag in my Jeep to clean them later so no DNA traces could be found. I wasn't going to risk setting anything else up, mainly out of concern that one of the homeless walking around might stumble in here after I picked the lock from the side garage door and took it with me before heading home.

When I got home, I showered and stayed up, reading a fantasy novel I'd preordered to pass the time. I still wasn't tired, but twenty-two pages in, I couldn't hold my focus any longer.

I turned on that *Mindhunter* show on Netflix, watching the fictionalization of nonfiction books. I'd read most of those books in college, and I wasn't fond of the author, largely because he had a habit of reminding the reader that he created something in the federal government. I begrudgingly gave it a chance, and it wasn't terrible. I actually liked the characters, which was a plus. It was also a good learning tool, the same as the books were. They told me how people slipped up and got caught.

I watched maybe four episodes of *Mindhunter* before my eyelids got droopy and I started to nod off. I turned the show off, and Minion huffed at me for trying to lie down and get into our usual sleep position for cuddles. She sat there, silently judging as she stared at me. I wiggled my way around until I was in the right spot. Minion gave me more shit, but she got under the comforter with me, and we cuddled our way to sleep, her eventually purring in my ear.

Saturday morning was here. Today was the day this would all go down. I ran through my plans over and over as I sat on my patio drinking coffee while Minion ate her breakfast. I spent more time this morning daydreaming in my pajamas. And why shouldn't I have? I'd waited months for this night, and I deserved it. I was nothing if not impatiently patient. t sucked, yet here I was today, finally able to do what I wanted more than anything. Alex would die tonight.

Twenty-Eight

I SPENT THE REST of the morning enjoying my coffee and the view. There was a man-made lake not far but not totally in view. Regardless, I was able to watch the ducks and other birds. It was the most peaceful morning I'd had since my last kill. Something told me tomorrow morning would be even more peaceful. It really didn't sit all that well with me that Osten would be losing one of his favorite employees, and I knew he'd ask me about what happened to Alex. Like with the cops, I couldn't tell him about killing the guy. I'd lie to him, too, and say I hadn't heard from Alex since he stormed from my house Thursday night after we had a fight about him acting like a jealous boyfriend. I could see how the cops would think that gave me reason to make the guy disappear, but really now, that was a lame reason. If they threw such allegations at me, I'd throw that stupidity back at them.

I'm not saying detectives were dumb. What I *am* saying is there are women who have killed for far less—ahem, Aileen Wuornos. Did you know she had an accomplice? Sorry, I'm babbling. I do that when I get excited.

As I finished my coffee, I heard a commotion over by the lake. It was a group of ducks squabbling with each other. From the looks of it, the males were fighting over the lone female, who made things worse by wiggling her tail feathers at the group. That was when the group started chasing her.

One large duck took the lead, and then the group was out of sight. I laughed at how much like humans those ducks were acting, or maybe it was the other way around. One female and a group of guys fighting over her. Such a damned shame that people held so much stock in relationships that they were willing to never see their own happiness through. I shrugged, picked up my mug, and went inside.

The clock on the microwave read 12:13 p.m. I couldn't believe that I had been out there that long. I thought it was only eight or so when I went out, but it was possible I was too sleepy and blurry to realize it may have been later. I still had a few hours to get ready for the party at Osten's house.

If I showed up early, I'd offer to help, but he'd admonish me. He made it clear that he hired people for these shindigs, and I'd made the mistake of offering to help one too many times.

Now I showed up anywhere between five and fifteen minutes late. Julie and I always "appeared" to arrive at the same time, kind of like a coincidence, but we planned it this time.

I still had a few hours to get ready. What was I going to do with myself? I was too excited and energetic to read or watch a movie. So, I went upstairs, changed, and went for a jog.

Bayshore was busy this time of day, and I didn't care one bit. I jogged to Sevendust, Marilyn Manson, Rob Zombie, Sixx A.M., and more rock bands. I even jogged and sang some Britney, NSYNC, and Backstreet Boys. This was my time, and nothing was going to dampen my excitement. Four miles up and the same amount back. I sweated like crazy because the sun was hot. It forced me to make a mental note to dress lightly for the party tonight.

I'd also pack clothes I wouldn't miss. They'd be burned along with everything else. Before I got in the shower, I stood in my closet, picking out outfits and putting them back. I finally settled on distressed jeans, wedges, and a red, partially sequined top.

I started the shower, threw my towels over the glass wall next to the shower door, opened the Pandora app, and turned on my Bluetooth speaker. I was ready to give the shower concert of a lifetime. I opened the door and stepped in, adjusting the temperature cooler because I'd sweated so much.

The first song to play was "Oops!...I Did It Again" by my namesake. I danced and sang my shower away, until all I had left was cold water. I felt better, too. I grabbed one towel and wrapped my hair in it; the other was for my body.

This time, Minion didn't try to cover me in fur, which I was thankful for. I glanced at the alarm clock, and it was only one-thirty. I still had four hours, plus the forty-five minutes—potential full hour—it took to do my makeup and hair. So, I left the towel in my hair and put a robe on. I still had no clue what I was going to do with all this energy.

Napping was out of the question, and I didn't want to jog again. So, I paced around my bedroom for a few minutes. Then, I paced downstairs. I forced myself onto the couch and tried to concentrate on horror movies. Those always seemed to get my attention. I chose DVDs over streaming—Rob Zombie's *House of 1,000 Corpses*, to be exact.

That killed two hours, but I still had two more. So, I threw in the original *Halloween*. Older movies were longer. Today's society had a hard time sitting still for anything over an hour and a half unless it was comic-book-related.

In a way, I supposed, my life could have been taken as a horror story. Though I suspect it would only be the killing parts. The rest of my day-to-day wasn't very active, and preferred it that way for obvious reasons.

Four hours down from watching horror movies. I forgot how easy it was to get lost in a horror marathon. I'd forgotten the towel was still in my hair, so I waited until I got upstairs to my bathroom to take it out. I hoped I didn't have a lot of frizz, but I had tamer and up-dos I could pull off if needed. Luckily, I needed neither and didn't even have to blow-dry it. I put my party clothes on, opened the safe and took out my supplies, pulled a bag from under my bed, and packed the supplies and a change of clothes. Then, I went back in the bathroom to put my makeup on.

I finished my makeup and double-checked the contents of the bag. Contractor bags, razors, rubber gloves, and a bottle of peroxide. I had a case of water in the back of my Jeep I could use to mix the with peroxide, but I still needed a bucket. I had one from Lowe's in the garage. I zippered the bag closed and headed downstairs.

Minion screamed at me, hungry since I'd missed her actual feeding time. I fed and petted her and made sure the front door was locked. I went out through the garage, picking the bucket up and placing the bag in it as the door opened. I opened the rear door on the Jeep and threw the bucket in and went back to the keypad for the garage and hit the button to close it. I also double-checked that I still had duct tape and found two rolls. All was well.

I walked to the driver door and settled in for the drive to Osten's party.

Twenty-Nine

I WAS GRATEFUL TRAFFIC was light—it meant there probably wouldn't be any on my way to the garage in Ybor, either. I hated that I'd be calling Alex at all—phone records would put me square in the sights of the cops, but it took about forty-eight hours to get those records. Not that the time mattered—because I already knew what I was going to tell them. Lies and bullshit were two other specialties of mine. When you rubbed shoulders with bigwigs for a living, you picked up new tricks and some of those were amazing. Take taxes, for example. I had the governor's own CPA on my client list. That man had saved my ass so many times, I felt like he was my personal financial savior.

I arrived at Osten's house ten minutes later, pulling up the U-shaped driveway to the valet waiting to take my Jeep and park it in the lot Osten had rented down the street. I slipped him a ten as I exited, and he climbed in. I wasn't worried about him finding anything in the back—these guys were paid for their discretion. Sometimes, for example, politicians and powerful CEOs came to these events, and the pretty, young things on their arms weren't their wives or husbands. The valets often argued over who got these jobs, knowing they were so lucrative around people with money to spend on silence.

I was greeted inside the front door by a server with a silver tray. The tray held glasses of champagne, red and white wines, and various cocktails. I grabbed a mojito and nodded to the server. They couldn't accept tips like the valets could. Instead, they were paid handsomely.

The food cost even more. Osten never cared about price. He rarely haggled over price, respecting that others were trying to run their own businesses as well. Meanwhile, I was here for food and appearances. And an alibi.

The house was well over five thousand square feet, had an open floor plan and sliding glass doors that opened to a meticulously manicured lawn, an in-ground pool with a hot tub and a water slide, and a flower garden to rival anything from the Tampa Garden Club.

I found Osten on the patio with the steel gazebo, near the gas fireplaces. He was holding a glass of whiskey and laughing at a joke someone told. He was surrounded by a "court" of current and future clients when he waved me over. I strode over next to him for our usual greeting, a hug and kiss on the cheek.

He introduced me. "For those of you who don't know, this is Britney Cage. She owns the greatest temp agency in town, and you'd be remiss if you didn't utilize her services." People nodded and raised their glasses to me, all saying hello.

I casually smiled, knowing at least two-thirds of them would ask for my card at some point. I'd brought plenty, and I was sure Julie had more. Osten asked me about Alex, and I told him we'd gotten into a fight and why. He was annoyed by that and said something about suspending Alex. I insisted he shouldn't be penalized at work for his personal life.

Osten was quick to note that if it wasn't for Alex's work life, he wouldn't even be in mine. I nodded my agreement and said no more. I knew when I was kicking the proverbial dead horse.

I excused myself from the group and was promptly followed by no less than four prospective clients. I shook their hands and gave them my card. We chatted briefly about their needs, and I asked them to call me, that I was looking for my assistant. I found her inside at the dining room table talking and eating. Of course, everyone was talking business; it was the easiest ice breaker.

I sat down next to Julie, eying her plate to see what kinds of barbecue were here. There was pulled pork, mac and cheese, brisket, coleslaw. I shivered at the sight of the cole slaw. It wasn't my kind of thing, and I love cabbage. My shiver caught Julie's eye, and she turned and hugged me.

"Speaking of my amazing boss, here she is," she said to a few people sitting across from her as she opened her hands Vanna White-style in my direction.

I stood to shake everyone's hands. "Hi, I'm Britney Cage." I sat back down, and we all chatted more about business, and I gave out more cards.

Julie stood to throw out her plate and asked me if I wanted anything. I asked her for some cornbread, if there was any, some pork, and a few slices of brisket. She smiled and went off to the kitchen.

A guy by the name of Brad something, a lawyer, was asking me all kinds of questions that I was more than happy to answer, but I felt like he was a sleaze lawyer, and I got the feeling I didn't want to work with him. So, instead of telling him to call, I told him how I vetted employees. He was enthusiastic about putting the practices to work and thanked me for my help.

Julie couldn't have come back soon enough. She handed me the plate and sat back down next to me. While I ate, I kept thinking that I needed to call Alex for my fake apology and our meet-up. But the food was so good, and the thoughts that followed the reminder to call him were those of killing him. I must've started smiling because I faintly heard someone joking that the food was "that good, huh?" I cleaned my plate in record time; even Julie was surprised.

"It's the first thing I've eaten all day," I said as I shrugged and excused myself. I allowed everyone to think I was going for more, even Julie. On my way to the kitchen, I pulled out my phone and called Alex. He answered, and I ran through my lies of being sorry and asked him to meet me at the garage. He agreed without hesitation. I was sure he'd be even more polite in person than on the phone. He apologized about five times in a three-minute conversation.

Appearances made, I kept an eye all around as I walked toward the door, making sure no one was really paying attention to me. I slipped out and handed the valet another ten, and he radioed for my Jeep. These guys were good; they even had the air on when they pulled it up for me. I got in and drove like a normal person would until I got to the main road out of the neighborhood. There was a gate, so speeding did me no good, but I drove five over anyway. The gate opened, and I pulled out slowly around the corner. Then I was off like a race car.

Thirty

I TOOK BACK ROADS, some through unsavory neighborhoods, but I was used to this. The garage was in one of those unsavory neighborhoods. I'd beaten Alex there and jumped out of my Jeep, leaving it running and the door open. I quickly put on a pair of rubber gloves, then opened the garage door enough to fit my Jeep in and closed it once I was inside. I turned the key to the off position and got out to change. I still had time before Alex was scheduled to arrive, and he was always on time, never early. I'd grown up with that saying "If you're early, you're on time, and if you're on time, you're late" or something like that, so I was always at least fifteen minutes early to meetings. It gave me time to prep. In this particular case, it was to change clothes and plan my luring of Alex with the promise of sex. Then, I'd chain him to the vehicle lift and kill him.

I paced the last four minutes I had until Alex would arrive. I checked every opening and every crack and hiding place, making sure no one else was here or could see in. The homeless were all a few blocks down, but that didn't really matter—they might wander this way, but they wouldn't hear a thing. Alex's mouth would be duct taped. All sound would be muffled, and they'd think nothing of it.

His car would be hidden in the dark by the garage door where I'd picked the lock. I would need to lock it back up after I loaded Alex's dead body in his trunk. I heard a car engine shut off and footsteps in the dead grass. Then he knocked; I smiled wickedly.

I pulled open the garage door and greeted Alex with a fake smile, stepping aside and welcoming him in.

He entered and I rolled the door back down. He kept walking, taking in the space. There was a confused look on his face. He obviously was worried about what was about to happen.

I walked over and hugged him. "I'm sorry for freaking out like that," I breathed in his ear, nibbling.

"Why are you apologizing? You were right to lose it on me." He pushed me back to arm's length, looking at me with love in his eyes.

I held back the bile that rose in the back of my throat.

"I acted like a jealous boyfriend, and I'm the one who should be groveling for forgiveness. Yet here you stand, ready to rip my clothes off and have your way with me. I'm certainly not going to complain. I'm just confused, I guess."

"I forgive you," I lied, pushing closer to him.

He let his elbows unlock and pulled me into him.

My plan was working. I kissed him hard, pushing him into the steel beam of the vehicle lift. He bit my lip in an unconscious response, apologizing again.

I pulled back, licked the blood from my lip, and devilishly smiled.

"Stay there. I want to try something," I told him as I picked up the chain and began wrapping it around him and the beam.

"This is some new kind of kink," he joked. "I like it."

In no time, I had him sort of hog-tied—the chain was around his ankles and shins, then up and around his wrists, hooked onto a screw on the arm. It was far enough away that Alex would be unable wriggle free from the lift.

I walked around the beam in a circle, looking at Alex like we were about to get into some dirty, kinky shit. Then I walked to my Jeep and took a pencil and roll of duct tape from a back compartment. As I came around, I put the pencil in my hair and pulled a piece of the duct tape off.

"Oh," Alex gulped, startled, "now we're really getting into it. I don't know that BDSM is my thing…"

"Don't worry." I smiled. "This won't take long."

I stepped forward and carefully placed the duct tape on his mouth. He tried to smile but couldn't. His eyes shone with excitement, and his little dick was standing at full attention. Clearly, he liked this.

I did, too, but not in the same way. I pulled the pencil out of my hair and ran the sharpened point along the side of his face. That was the moment he realized this was some fucked-up kind of kink he didn't want any part of. I didn't say anything—just laughed—as he squirmed and tried to break free. I ran the pencil down the other side of his face, still smiling and laughing.

I leaned into his right ear and in a husky voice said, "This is what happens when you're too polite for your own good. Consider this a mercy. Consider it my…my gift to you, you little fucking worm." His little cock, which had been rock hard in my gloved hand, instantly shrank.

I pulled my face back and brought the pencil down hard and clear into his ear canal, slamming it through his ear drum and lodging it in his right temporal lobe.

His eyes were wide with shock, and his head lulled lazily. I didn't bother to pull the pencil out. His body started to seize as his jaw clapped up and down like he was trying to say something. His last words maybe?

I laughed and walked back up to him, leaning down again. "What's that? Oh? You're sorry? Oh, Alex, I know you are." I slapped him as hard as I could across his useless fucking face. Then I leaned back in a final time. "But I'm not."

I kept laughing as Alex slipped away, then I went to work grabbing the contractor bags from my Jeep and placing one over his head, securing it around his neck with duct tape. I made sure there were no leaks by running the duct tape around three times.

Next, I unhooked the chain and unwound it from Alex's feet and wrists, throwing it in another contractor bag, then into the back of my Jeep. I didn't want to risk the peroxide eating through the bag, so I planned to clean the chain in the bucket at some out-of-the-way, middle-of-nowhere type spot on the way back from dumping the body. There were plenty of those along the way, especially taking back roads.

I hoisted Alex over my shoulder before he could fall to the ground. He was heavy, but I had expected that. I put my arm between his legs and grabbed the back of his pants to make sure I had a good hold and wouldn't drop him.

I leaned him up against the wall next to the roll-up door and hoisted the door open. I searched his pockets for his keys, and when I found them, I jogged to his car and opened the trunk. Back to the garage I walked, and back over my shoulder Alex went. There was no lighting for anyone to see me carrying a body, and if anyone had seen, well, he was my drunk friend. That would work. I placed him down carefully; I didn't want the bag to rip prematurely and get blood and cerebrospinal fluid everywhere.

When I was certain Alex's body was secure, I closed the trunk lid. I then went back into the garage to make sure I didn't miss anything. I grabbed the bucket, putting the peroxide, bottles of water and chain inside, but I saw nothing else I'd missed. Maybe my earlier anxiety had been misplaced

Before I locked and armed my Jeep, I grabbed more rubber gloves, putting a new pair on immediately so I didn't leave prints. After pulling the roll-up door back down, I locked it back up with the same lock I'd picked. I had tools with me to pick it again. For now, I had to get this body across the state and into that mud pit.

Getting into the driver's seat of Alex's car, I fell in, which made me wonder why he drove a car so low to the ground. I had to move the seat up a few inches and adjust the mirrors. I carefully backed out onto the street, stopping to look at the paper map I'd stashed in a pocket, noting I had to make a right onto East Adamo and stay on that all the way across.

I'd stop again to check the map because there were a few other turns, and I didn't want to hit I-95. I turned the radio to a rock station and hit the gas.

Thirty-One

I DROVE FOR ALMOST one hundred miles before pulling off at a rest stop to check the map again. I had memorized the turns to the place with the tank. I could've used GPS, but that was a dumb idea given cops' ability to pull any tracking data on me they wanted. Smashing Alex's phone had been equally dumb, given I knew they'd pull the records and question me anyway, but I wasn't going to make it easy on them by opening up a GPS on any phone even remotely connected to my name. I was about thirty minutes out, and I was starting to come down from my high; it would come back once I got to the dump site. On I drove, until I pulled up to the tank place I scanned with the flashlight on my phone for the mud area and found it quicker than expected. It was off to the right about five hundred feet.

I turned the headlights off and cruised at low speed until I got the car where I wanted it and popped the trunk. I hoisted Alex out and carried him to the mud. As I expected, there were footprints everywhere, so mine would blend in and be impossible to isolate. I dropped the body into the obvious path of the tanks and started peeling the duct tape from around his neck. Luckily, I didn't notice any marks or missing skin, so I could only hope forensics would lead nowhere with that. After I pulled the bag from Alex's head, I pulled the pencil out of his ear. A trickle of pink blobbed out and ran down his face—cerebrospinal fluid mixed with blood ruined my elation at blood in the moonlight.

There would be more killings for that, though. Putting the pencil in the bag with the duct tape, I used my feet to smush his body into the mud enough that no one would notice until he got caught up in the tracks of a tank.

Looking around to see that there was nothing else I needed to do, I turned toward the lump of Alex's body in the mud. "I should have killed you more slowly. You gave up way too easily. Just like the pathetic little bitch you were." I kicked at his head and got a jolt of fresh excitement from the impact. "Rest in piss, fuckface."

I walked back to Alex's car and drove back the way I'd come. I stopped on the side of State Road 60 to burn the remaining evidence and clean the chain. I burned every-thing—duct tape, used gloves after putting another pair on, the pencil of death, everything—as I cleaned the chain in the peroxide water. Once the chain was clean, I threw it in another contractor bag and set the bucket on fire. I was sad to see it go, but another would only cost about five dollars, so I wasn't going to bitch about it. All the evidence needed to go, and that was that.

When I got back to Ybor, I drove past the garage my Jeep was parked in and over to the junkyard with the crusher a few blocks away. I pulled in, paid one of the guys who worked there with a hundred-dollar bill that guaranteed that he'd never seen me and that he'd immediately add this car to be crushed.

Then I took the bag with the chain out. On my walk back to the garage, I took the gloves off and put them in my pocket. There was something else in the pocket. I reached in and pulled out a razor. I had prepped pretty well, considering I didn't even need the razor. I'd use it again; of that I was sure.

Carrying this chain in a bag made me almost look like one of the homeless I didn't see. I kept walking, knowing it was late and they were most likely asleep, and when I looked to my left, I saw their tent city. I exhaled relief and took a right toward the garage door where my Jeep was waiting for me.

I went and picked the lock, rolled up the door, and climbed into my Jeep. After I backed out, I pulled the door back down and placed the lock back on. I got back into my Jeep and drove the speed limit so I wouldn't be noticed. I glanced at the clock on my dash. It was 4:37 a.m. Thankfully, today was Sunday, though I didn't consider it the next day until I'd gone to sleep and woken up again. Not that it mattered.

I was euphoric; my heart rate when I killed Alex was the same as my resting rate. The only time it rose was with the physical exertion of carrying him. Still, I wasn't going to fall asleep anytime soon.

I took my time driving home, all through back roads. I was in no hurry, and I wanted to enjoy the dark before the dawn. By the time I got home, only half an hour had gone by. There had been no traffic to deal with; I'd had the roads all to myself.

I walked in my front door, and Minion half mewed at me, stretching and judging me for being gone all night. It may have been close to her breakfast feeding, but she hadn't been fed the night prior, so I fed her right away and went upstairs to shower and lay in bed, watching something I'd already seen a hundred times, until I fell asleep. Minion came up after finishing her food; I was finishing my shower. I got out and dried off, still feeling tingly

When I woke up later, I planned to bring the Jeep into the garage and empty out what was left inside. I wanted to wash it, too. It hadn't been for a few months, and I usually had a detailer handle it, particularly because I didn't have the patience to hand wax it. I set a reminder in my phone to call the detailer on Monday to make an appointment.

Minion almost tripped me as I put my pajamas on and jumped on the bed as I tried to pull the comforter down. She screamed at me as she sat there looking pathetic and unloved. I shook my head and laughed, moving her as I climbed in. I hit play on one of the Jurassic Park movies and Minion curled up in her spot, purring softly. We fell asleep in minutes.

When I woke, I looked at the angry alarm clock—1:14 p.m. I got out of bed and went downstairs to get my newspaper and start a pot of coffee. Julie called, asking if I wanted to do lunch.

"I'm not hungry, but I did just start a pot of coffee if you'd like to come over."

"That sounds nice. I'll be there soon."

Awesome. I may as well back the Jeep inside now and wash it when she leaves. Or I can run it through one of those brush- less things. No. I'll just wait until I call the detailer tomorrow.

I didn't bother to change; Julie had seen me in pajamas before. I went out through the garage, grabbing the paper, and backing my Jeep in. I'd just closed the garage door when my doorbell rang.

"Just a minute!" I yelled.

I didn't bother walking too fast because I was sure Julie would be fine. I didn't even check the peephole to make sure it was Julie. I unlocked and opened the door. I wasn't paying attention to who was standing there—a patrol car caught my attention first. When I looked up, the officer had "the look" on his face. The one where they have to give you bad news. I immediately thought something happened to Julie.

"Hello, Officer. How may I help you?"

"Ms. Cage?"

"Yes. Would you like to come in?"

"If you don't mind, yes. I'm afraid I have some troubling news for you."

I opened the door farther to let him in. He stuck his hand out as he stepped inside. "Officer Sweet. Nice to finally meet you."

Oh shit.

Thirty-Two

I USHERED HIM INTO the kitchen, offering him some coffee as I poured my own. He politely declined. I tried to make small talk until Julie arrived. At one point, I even asked him outright if he could wait a few minutes for Julie to get here. He agreed and sat at the table. I sat with him, staring into the endless black depth in a mug. The doorbell rang, ripping me from the swimming my brain was doing. *Am I caught? What's going on? At least it's not Julie. If it was, he'd have told me, instead of letting me wait for her.* Whatever he had to tell me must've been bad; the look on his face saddened then hardened as I yelled that it was open. Julie came running to my side. I looked at Sweet, who introduced himself to Julie.

Julie sat in the chair next to me, and I nodded at Sweet, indicating I was as ready as I could be to hear what he had to say.

He cleared his throat. "Like I said, I have some troubling news. Dr. Joe Osten had a heart attack while driving to play golf this morning. He asked that we notify you in person. His children have already been called. You should get to the hospital as soon as you can, Ms. Cage."

A tear dropped from my face into my coffee. Then another and another, until I was full-on crying. Through my tears,

I managed to ask what hospital, and Julie escorted Officer Sweet out.

I sipped my coffee, trying to keep my cool, but I cried as I did. Teardrop martinis had been a thing on a TV show I loved, but teardrop coffee wasn't as appetizing.

Julie came back to me and was talking, but I didn't hear her. I was staring off into the lake. She gently tapped my shoulder; I turned my tear-stained face to her. She said she was driving and that I needed to change and brush my teeth. Julie helped me upstairs, picked out track pants and a T-shirt, while I brushed. I changed in a haze. The man who was like a second father to me, the man I thought invincible. This couldn't be real.

Julie helped me down the stairs and into her car. She drove to me Tampa General and didn't leave me alone, except when I went into Osten's room. He was awake, fiddling with the TV remote. I ran over to the side of the bed and hugged him.

He held me for what felt like a long time; I cried into his chest. I couldn't lose him. Not that he knew I left his party last night and killed one of his employees, but he was like family. I picked my head up and sat back into an upright position, wiping the tears from my face.

Osten smiled at me, putting a hand on my leg.

"I don't understand. I thought your cardiologist said you were fine?"

"He did. Six months ago. I haven't exactly been taking care of myself, Brit. I almost expected this."

"Joe, why? Why would you risk leaving your biological children, your business you love so much…me?"

"I want to enjoy my life without restrictions. I see now that I can't. I don't want to leave you kids until I'm ready. And I'm not ready right now. Tomorrow they're going to put a stent or two in. and I'll be good as new.

"Of course, I'll have to close the office until I can perform surgery again. It'll only be a couple of weeks, so I'll drop to a skeleton crew. Everyone still gets paid, and those who work will get extra vacation time." He talked as though nothing was wrong, that he didn't have to face his own mortality. But that's just who he was. Dr. Joseph S. Osten wouldn't have had it any other way.

He went back to flipping through the channels while I walked out and told Julie what was going on. I told her I might take some time off to help him with his recovery, if he let me.

Knowing him, a nurse would be at his house, and he'd insist I start making contracts out of those connections from his party. I chuckled in spite of the scare.

Julie and I walked back into his room in time to see a breaking news headline. The body of a man had been found at that place you can drive a tank in the mud or over cars. I faked a gasp when everyone else's was real. The reporter went on to say the man's shirt had gotten caught and wrapped up between the wheel and track of the tank, bringing the body to the surface. A deputy on scene was being interviewed, saying things like "Looks like a man in his twenties…" and "ID not yet confirmed…"

"Who could do such a thing," Julie asked, putting a hand over her mouth.

"Someone sick," Osten replied.

I am not sick, dammit. So, Alex had been found. A little earlier than I'd hoped, but that was okay. I was ready for the cops to start asking questions. Officer Sweet would either be on the opposite end of the phone or in my office by the end of the week. He wouldn't be able to question Osten until after

his recovery, and besides, the man knew nothing. He knew Alex left work Friday night and that was it.

I, on the other hand, was the only one who knew what happened. And I would forever be the only one to know.

We stayed with Osten until dinner, when we were sworn by his nurses to not go get him outside food. When they brought his dinner, we decided to get dinner ourselves. I was still in a bit of a haze from almost losing him, but Julie was a huge help. I could never begin to properly thank her. That girl was my rock.

Julie handed the bit of card stock to the valet. While we waited, I started to talk to her.

"Julie, I don't know if I'll ever be able to properly thank you for being my rock today…"

"Stop it. You'd do the same for me, and I know it. I'm being a good friend—"

She was cut off by my phone going off, one person after another calling. I switched it to silent. I didn't need or want to talk to anyone else.

"Now, please finish what you were saying before my phone rudely interrupted," I said to her.

"Nothing, I was just saying you'd do the same for me, that's all. Let's go get some dinner, then I'll take you home?"

I nodded as the valet brought Julie's car up. She put her hand on my shoulder, then tipped the valet before we got in. She drove for what felt like hours.

We wound up going to Denny's, which was pretty perfect. Julie knew I loved greasy food when I was stressed out, and this was the perfect time. I ordered a huge breakfast meal, knowing I'd be taking half of it home. Julie ordered a few eggs, bacon, and hash browns.

Neither of us seemed to be in the mood for actual dinner. It was only seven, but we didn't care. We didn't talk for a long time, even after the waitress came and took our orders and brought our coffee. I just stared at the table, and Julie watched me.

The waitress came back with our food, we thanked her and dug in. We even ate in silence, which we'd never done before. It was a strange feeling. I felt bad, and I felt Julie did, too.

She finally broke the silence. "So, do you want to go home from here or maybe do something?"

"I think I wanna go home. Wanna have a sleepover? I know it's a work night, but I could sure use more than Minion around tonight."

"Of course! We can swing by my place on the way to yours."

I smiled and put my hand on hers, tearing up again. I hadn't even feel sadness over losing my mom; she hadn't been part of my life for a long time before I cut her out of it like some hoebag teenager in a slasher flick.

We finished what we could and boxed the rest. Julie wouldn't let me pay, so I tried to leave the tip, but she didn't allow that, either. We got back in her car and headed for home.

Thirty-Three

WHEN WE GOT BACK to my house, I fed Minion after she begged Julie for pets, and Julie and I went up to my room. I'd grabbed a bottle of wine before I left the kitchen, and we showered, changed, and drank from the bottle in bed. We watched movies until the bottle was empty and we passed out from being so tired. I don't recall ever feeling so exhaust-ed from caring about someone so much, but here I was, beat from crying over almost losing Osten. My eyes had felt as though they would fall out before I fell asleep.

Julie and I awoke the next morning initially not knowing where we were. I rubbed the sleep from my eyes and looked around. At some point, we'd made our way back downstairs. We'd fallen asleep on my couch, one of us at either end.

I got up to make coffee, while Julie went to the bathroom. I started the pot and ran upstairs to the master bath. Minion chased me, cutting in front of me halfway up, almost tripping me, like cats like to do.

I brushed my teeth and washed my face. My eyes were so puffy they hurt. I wanted to be by Osten's side—his biological kids couldn't make it down, and I was the closest thing he had here. I knew he'd tell me to get back to work. Even better, he wouldn't know Alex was missing either for a week, when he reopened his office or when the cops came knocking.

I had a tingle on the back of my neck; they would call me long before they called Osten. Or would they? Did it even matter?

At the moment, nothing mattered to me other than Osten. When I got back downstairs, Julie had already poured us both coffee and was sitting at the table waiting for me, my mug at my seat. I thanked her as I sat down. We sipped in silence for a while.

Julie broke it first. "Have you called him yet?"

"No. I want to go see him, but I know what he'll say. He'll tell us not to worry and go to work. That's just the type of person he is. And when they let him off his leash, he'll have a home nurse for a few days, probably one of his employees, and he'll give them an extra week PTO." I shook my head and sipped my coffee.

"So, are we going in today?"

"I don't think so. Everything will still be there tomorrow. If you want to go home to Cody, don't let me stop you. I'll probably just lie around with tea bags on my puffy-ass eyes."

Julie laughed. "I'll probably be doing the same thing. Cody has class today and work tonight, but I should call him and let him know we're all okay."

"Go ahead. I'm going to call Osten real quick and see if he needs anything anyway," I said as I stood up to grab my phone from the coffee table.

Julie chatted away with Cody while I called Osten's room. He admonished me as only a father could, telling me I needed to go to work today, blah, blah, blah. I let all that go in one ear and out the other. I wasn't planning to tell him that Julie and I were going to hang around in our pajamas all day, resting our swollen eyes and exhausted souls. I reassured him I was okay, and we hung up. I poured both of us more coffee and toasted a few bagels.

We ate at the coffee table, watching *Good Morning America*, and laughed at each other when we asked, in unison, if it was too early to drink. The *was* Florida after all. Day drinking was a real thing, even when people were at their jobs. I've seen it. We treated the rest of the day like a spa day, then we ordered pizza, Julie going home after dinner. I went to bed buzzed and happier than the night before.

The week Osten went back to work was when things got hairy in the ways I'd expected. He'd noticed Alex missing, and I was the first one he called, naturally. The last Osten knew, Alex was staying with me while his place was being repaired from the toaster oven fire. When the news showed the tank place, the cops only said they were waiting for an ID.

That ID had eventually been made, and since no one really knew whom to contact, the cops went right to Osten. Alex's place of employment was the only thing they could find. I told him Alex and I made up, but we hadn't spoken since our apologies, and those were over the phone.

Then Officer Sweet came by the office to talk to me about that, something about I'd been the last number he'd spoken to. I told him the same thing: Alex had stayed with me while his place was being fixed, we had an argument about him acting like a jealous boyfriend, and I called him to apologize, while he admitted he was in the wrong. I told Sweet that Alex and I moved past it and left our relationship in the friend zone. I also told him I hadn't heard from Alex since, which was the only bit of truth aside from the jealousy thing.

Sweet seemed momentarily suspicious but apparently determined I was too nice a person—too accommodating—to do something like what had been done to Alex. If he only knew. I walked him out of the office and wished him a safe shift. When I came back in, Julie looked at me funny.

"What's up?"

"There's something weird about that cop."

"Weird? Like what?"

"I can't figure it out, but it's like he doesn't trust anyone. Like, when he first came in talking about Osten, it seemed like he suspected Osten himself. Maybe the guy is reaching for clues in the dark, I don't know. He just seems…off."

"He is reaching in the dark. I know I was the last person to talk to Alex, but did it ever occur to anyone that maybe the dude killed himself? Not that the news or Sweet told us much, but from the sounds of it, Alex could've done that all alone. Maybe he wanted to die. None of us knew if he had any mental illness, and that's not even our business. Sweet knows he needs to cover all angles with this. And he can't pin it on me all over a phone call."

"So, you're banking on being acquitted on circumstantial evidence?" Julie joked.

"Yes, yes I am." We laughed as I walked back into my office. So far, I'd succeeded. I'd thrown the cops off my trail, but I knew Sweet would come back.

I couldn't kill him; he was a fucking cop, and the department knew what he was up to. That would have been just stupid.

If he came calling again, I'd throw him off again. It might be a long cycle, but I didn't really care. Any evidence the cops might come up with would be circumstantial, and Florida juries loved to acquit when it was only circumstantial—just ask that girl in Orlando.

At any rate, I had work to be done, and I had dinner plans with the girls. Julie was now part of that group, and she enjoyed it. We were more than happy to have her.

Julie and I finished our work and drove separate vehicles to our dinner spot.

Thirty-Four

JULIE WAS REALLY FITTING in with the group, which was something she'd always wanted—a group of friends to hang out with whom she could confide in. I was just glad she wanted to be seen with us. Sometimes we were a bit much, kind of like a bunch of teenagers. We were fun, though, and caring. If she ever needed anything, we had her covered. She also had a full set of bridesmaids now. Our current conversation consisted of talking about the most hideous bridesmaid gowns we'd ever worn, complete with photos. We passed each other's phones around, until mine was handed back to me. It was ringing, and I recognized the number this time.

"Yes, Officer Sweet. How can I help you?"

"I'm sorry. Did I catch you at a bad time?"

"Nope, just having dinner with some friends. What can I do for you?"

"This is very unprofessional of me, but I was wondering if you'd like to join me for dinner one evening. Not to thank you, but because I'm interested in you."

Well then, talk about setting a girl back on her heels. I thought about it for a moment and replied, "As long as you understand that I'm not interested in a relationship, though I will agree to friends with benefits. If the sex isn't good, I won't stick around, either."

The girls had hushed their conversation and were now watching me and giggling. They'd all heard this before. Well, all of them except Julie; she blushed overhearing this conversation.

"I'm okay with that," Sweet agreed. I wondered if he was now just trying to get into my house and Jeep, thinking I killed Alex. Was he undercover now? I'd keep my guard up, and he'd never come to my house.

My Jeep had already been fully detailed, and all of my supplies were locked in a hidden compartment of my gun safe. I'd installed it myself over the previous weekend. I knew the shit storm headed my way, and I also knew how to cut it off at the knees. Sweet and I didn't make plans right then, though I did tell him I'd call him tomorrow, and we hung up.

I'd rather err on the side of caution. He's never coming over; I'm never driving anywhere unless it's in his vehicle. I know my rights, and I know that my Jeep is clean. Everything in it's used for rock climbing. They'd be morons to search it. Besides, I do have the best lawyer in town; he'll get it thrown out on technicalities.

Sarah broke into my thoughts, asking when my next crawling day was. I realized it was this upcoming weekend. She asked to join me.

I asked if she was squeamish. We made plans for her to stay with me Monday night, since I was headed out Tuesday morning. The crawl was in Tennessee, and I wanted to get plenty of rest before the weekend's events started. The event itself ran Wednesday through Saturday, so that was an entire week off for me.

Julie was nervous, but I was excited for her. I knew she'd be able to handle this. Maybe I'd start going on more crawl events. Hell, maybe I'd take actual vacations. I wasn't sure yet, and I wanted Julie to be comfortable with being in the office alone.

We finished dinner and shared another two bottles of wine between us while we talked and caught up on each other's lives. All the kids were doing well in school, and the husbands were also doing well. During these conversations, I wondered what it would be like to have one—a husband—then I realized that would be another person I'd have to lie to, and I didn't want to deal with that. Husbands were just grown-up versions of kids, too. At least, that's what my friends kept telling me. And I'd seen a lot of it for myself in photos they'd post on social media.

The server brought all our checks. We paid and parted ways, promising to do this again soon.

Julie and I chatted on the walk to our vehicles, largely about her running the office while I was out for a week. I assured her she'd be fine; she disagreed. It was nerves talking, I knew, so I'd schedule motivational emails and texts. I also reminded her she could call me whenever she needed to. Phone service would be sketchy, but I'd call her back no matter what.

When I got home, I scheduled those daily emails and texts. Julie would love them. The first email included letting her know that Cody was more than welcome to hang with her in the office if she wanted. I knew she'd find it unprofessional, but it was the thought that counted, right? I had all confidence in her. I had to keep reminding her that if I didn't, I wouldn't leave her alone for a few days, let alone a whole week. She was excited and terrified at the same time. I smiled as I hit Schedule on the last email and picked up my phone.

I called Sweet, and he invited me over. I accepted for obvious reasons. He was a good-looking guy, muscular, black hair, green eyes, tan, and loved to run marathons. The jogger in me wanted us to spend "real" time together, not just sex. The rest of me screamed "absolutely not!"

I still didn't know if he was genuinely interested in me or still trying to rule me out as a suspect and would have a team search my Jeep while I slept. I decided to let the chips fall where they may. I'd spend the night a few times, which he'd have anticipated if I were still a suspect. The thought made me uneasy, but I was me, and while I might let him fuck me, there was no way in hell I'd let that man fuck with my confidence.

I fed Minion, grabbed a toothbrush, and left.

The sex was better than good; I'd have been lying if I said otherwise. He tried to get to know me better while we lay together, my head on his shoulder. I led the conversation with my answers, learning more about him than he did me. The most I'd allowed before we fell asleep was that I was an only child who was incredibly driven throughout high school and college, taking myself to where I am today.

He was okay with my refusal to open up any further; whether that was because he was now sleeping with a suspect or out of genuine respect for me as a person, I didn't know. *How do you ask if you're still a suspect without sounding like a suspect, anyway?*

I awoke in the morning, brushed my teeth, and let myself out. I didn't know his work schedule and didn't think to ask last night. We'd worn each other out, giving me about three hours' sleep. I checked my Jeep to make sure everything was as I'd left it last night. It was. I was very specific about what went where; organized yet chaotic at times. I walked back around and climbed into the driver's seat.

Minion lost her little mind on me when I got home. I hadn't been there for her to sleep in my hair or cuddle with, and for her, that was world ending. I fed her and ran up the stairs to shower the sex stink off and get ready for work. I decided to put my makeup on once I got to the office. I was already running late.

By the time I walked into the office, it was 10:16 a.m. Julie looked up at me, laughed and blushed, and looked back down at her computer. I could hear the giggles as I walked past her into my office. I set my things down, taking out my makeup bag, and walked into my private bathroom. As I was putting said makeup on, Julie came in wanting to know how last night went.

"Well, I'm over an hour late. You tell me." I smirked and went back to evening my mascara.

Julie laughed and went back to her desk. I realized she and I needed to go over a few things over the next couple of days since I was leaving in four.

But then my cell rang—Sweet. I let him go to voice mail. I had no intention of leading him on, but I wasn't in a mood to talk to him yet. He was probably upset that I didn't wake him before I left. Oh well. He'd get over it.

As good as the sex was, I wasn't about to make him a regular booty call. He was a cop, I was a killer, end of story. I would lie a little more, telling him he was not the only one I was sleeping with, that I was clean, and also that he couldn't act like I was his girl because that would make me cut him off faster than Lorena Bobbitt cut of her husband's dick.

I'd break it off with him when I got back from Tennessee. For the remaining three days, I'd fuck him at least once, and enjoy it.

I didn't have to plan an itinerary for Sarah and me because most of the trip was Jeep-related events. I needed it, and so did my Jeep. She needed to get some mud on her, surrounded by mountains and beautiful views and other Jeep owners.

Sure, we had Tampa Jeep clubs, but we really only had mud holes; no climbing, except out of a hole if we got stuck. I only needed to plan where we were stopping for food. Then again, Sarah wasn't too fussy about road trip food, so we could really stop anywhere that was open. I knew we'd go to Walmart or somewhere the night before we left for snacks and drinks; we'd stock up like unsupervised children in the candy and chips aisles.

The day ended, bringing me one more day closer to a girls' trip. Sarah was going to get out of her house. She had no desire to be home alone while her husband took her son hunting for gator.

I was already halfway packed. I needed to do some laundry, and that would be it. Julie was going to stay at my house and take care of Minion, largely because Minion was picky and she really liked Julie. On my drove home, I called Sweet back.

"Hey! What's up?"

"Not much. Just headed home to get some laundry done for the Jeep trip. You called, and I didn't want to be rude and not call back. What's going on?"

"I wanted to let you know we hit a dead end with Alex's investigation. No one knows anything, and if I can't prove, without a doubt, that someone killed him, I have to let it go cold. My bosses hate low close rates, so the sooner this closes, the better. Not that unsolved are any better than cold…"

"Aww, I'm sorry. I really wish I had something for you. But you are aware that since we had sex, you'd have to recuse yourself from the investigation, right?"

"Stop that. I know the rules around my job. And, yes, I know that. I'd do it now, but I'd like to give whatever is going on between us a little longer. I'm not recusing myself over a one-night stand. If you don't tell, why would I?"

"And if your superiors found out anyway, you'd be fucked. Just recuse yourself."

"Are you saying *you'd* tell?"

"No," I lied. "I'm simply saying you called when I was around my friends. I'm not going to hush them."

"Fair enough. You do have a point. If one of my neighbors wants to be an asshole, they could. I do have a few who'd do almost anything to get me thrown off a case or off the force."

"Anyone willing to stoop to that level over petty bullshit deserves all the bad karma they can get."

We laughed. "All right, I'm home. I have to go, but I'll call you when I get back."

"Okay. Drive safe and have a fun trip."

He terminated the call before I did.

Thirty-Five

Julie and I went over some last-minute things that needed to be done around the office, and I let her run through payroll while I watched. Not like a hawk, just a casual observer. I pointed out tips and tricks, and she jotted them down in her notebook. That notebook was filled with things she'd learned since I hired her. She even noted things I did and said so she could interact and play the game with the clients like a pro. And she really was. I was impressed with how quickly she'd picked up everything. I was confident and comfortable leaving her to run Passing Through while I was gone.

Friday came and went without a call or text from Sweet. At least until about ten p.m. My text alert went off. Sweet told me his superiors ordered Alex's case closed, no ifs, ands, or buts about it. This was the end.

Sweet was relieved, but he was also ready to recuse himself. It occurred to me that I'd never paid attention to what his first name was, but he wasn't the first fuck whose name I was fuzzy on. His card was at the office, so I texted him back saying that it might be a good thing they wanted it closed and asked him his first name. He laughed with that emoji that had tears on either side and looked like it was rolling.

"Come on. Cut me a break. Your card is in my desk at the office," I responded.

"John."

"Well, John, it's nice to officially meet you," I replied, including the same emoji he'd just sent.

"Does this mean we can be more than—never mind. I'm sorry. I don't know why I asked that. Forgive me?"

"Forgiven, but please don't do it again." I added a smiley face, so he'd know I wasn't actively trying to be a bitch.

"Done."

"Great. Well, I'll text you when I get back. I'm sure I'll have some extra energy to burn." Emoji weren't needed this time; he knew what I meant.

Minion and I did laundry and finished packing for my trip. While we waited for the washer and dryer, we'd watch movies or read books. It was a true "Netflix and chill" night, not what kids these days make it out to be.

I was supposed to have finished the laundry yesterday, but I'd gone for a jog instead. Something about Sweet—John—made me want to work out with him, like at the gym and jog. We weren't friends, just sexual partners with no strings. The fact that my brain—or was it my brain?—might want something else was unacceptable. *That's* why I'd gone for that jog.

With the laundry finally finished, I could pack and have a clear head. Julie would be coming over tomorrow to get the spare key and learn Minion's feeding quirks. She was one spoiled cat. She ate nowhere other than the countertop, drank fresh filtered water from a glass. All she needed was a crown she wouldn't wear. I'd still find one small enough and try. That was just me.

Minion and I lay down on the couch, her in my lap, a book in my hands. The next thing I knew, the book was on my face, and Minion stirred as if to ask why I dared disturb her. It was midnight. Minion was fed, and I headed off to shower and sleep…or try to.

I wasn't quite awake during my shower, so I hoped I'd be able to go back to sleep once I lay in bed. That wasn't happening. *Would it be tacky if I booty-called John?*

He came over, and we had great sex. The sun was starting to rise as we'd finished, so I made coffee before kicking him out. Luckily, I didn't have to. He had work in a few hours. We sat in silence, enjoying the beautiful sky and coffee, neither of us telling the other how much we enjoyed each other s company. He kissed me on the cheek as he left.

A few hours later, Julie came over. We ran through everything she needed to know; I even left her the phone number to where Sarah and I were staying for the event. All emergency numbers on the fridge…I didn't want to sound like a mom leaving her teenager home alone for the first time.

Julie left and I made one last single meal. It was a nice feeling. I was looking forward to this trip, and I knew Sarah was too.

Sarah and I made it to Tennessee, checked into the hotel, dropped our bags in our room, and went off to check in for the events. The woman running check-in was cheerleader happy, and everyone was super friendly. It was nice to be surrounded by those who enjoyed the sport. Mostly my friends thought it was crazy how I'd do something "so dangerous." It always made me laugh when they said that.

Just before dinner, I called Osten to see how he was feeling. He'd sent the nurse home and reopened the office. He mentioned he'd called Julie to find a replacement for Alex, lamenting the loss. We'd all supposed Alex got mixed up in something he shouldn't have, but none of us could fathom it. I wished him well and hung up.

Julie would find someone better for Osten's office. Alex was my mistake. I swore I'd never do that again.

When we got back to Tampa, I'd agreed to go to the local gym with John. The place had these rules about being obnoxious while working out and making all kinds of noise and judging others.

I was fit, sure, and so was John, but then there were the gym rats, the meatheads. They were giants of men—six feet tall at a minimum, but with all that bulk, they couldn't wipe their own asses if they tried. Then there were their chicken legs, completely out of place against the girth of their ripped upper bodies. These dudes clearly didn't like leg day. They were a special kind of rude asshole. *My* kind of rude asshole that I liked teaching a lesson to. *I think I've uncovered another reason.*

Acknowledgments

This book, let alone series, wouldn't be possible without the following people and references:

Practical Homicide Investigation (5th Edition) by way of a Thomas Harris acknowledgement. The FBI's *Serial Murder Multi-Disciplinary Perspectives for Investigators* Report (available free online), and *psychologytoday.com* for helping me add the necessary depth to Britney.

Ret. Sgt. Chuck Burns for his consultation where the textbook didn't answer specific questions.

Justin D., for helping me on ridiculously short notice with some nicknames.

Nathan, for his advice and invitations. I'm so very grateful I finally decided to take you up.

Mark…sweet Mark. Without you, I wouldn't be here. I love you more than I can express and always will.

Jason, for the awesome editing and blurbs and feedback and advice and just being you. You have made me the writer I am today. Let's not get arrested, please. At least not before we make that money.

Also by
Amanda Byrd

13 Reasons for Murder:
Politeness Kills (#1)
Meathead (#2)
Philistines (#3)
Hungry (#4)
Bad Blood (#5)
Betrayal (#6)
Disillusioned (#7)
Harlot (#8) *2023*

The Morgan Davis Serials
The Girl at the Bottom of the Ocean (#1)
Before You Die (#2)

Anthologies
Thrill of the Hunt: Cabin Fever (Thrill of the Hunt Anthology
Book 6)